CHEERLEADERS

#28

SCHEMING

LISA NORBY

SCHOLASTIC INC.
New York Toronto London Auckland Sydney

ISBN 0-590-40633-7

12 11 10 9 8 7 6 5 4 3 2 1   7 8 9/8 0 1 2/9

Printed in the U.S.A.   01

First Scholastic printing, April 1987

CHEERLEADERS

SCHEMING

CHEERLEADERS

CHAPTER

1

"*May I have the envelope, please. . . .*"

Robert Redford looked earnestly into the TV camera. "This is the moment we've all been waiting for, ladies and gentlemen. And the winner is . . . the young actress who gave such a marvelous performance in her debut film, that dazzling new star — Tara Armstrong!"

Tara let out a shriek of joy and planted a kiss on the cheek of the handsome young man in a dinner jacket sitting next to her. As she made her way to the podium to accept her Oscar, the spotlights followed her progress. Her wonderful gown, simply cut but covered from neck to hem in silver sequins, shimmered magically under the lights. Tears glistened in her eyes. She was overcome with the thrill of the moment. But not too overcome to notice the envious looks on the faces of

1

the nominees she had just edged out to win the award for best actress: Meryl Streep, Ally Sheedy, Jessica Lange. . . .

"Tara, for Pete's sake, will you stop hogging that mirror and let someone else have a chance!"

The voice belonged to a Jessica all right. But not to Jessica Lange.

Tara turned and faced Jessica Bennett. "Okay, I'll move. But you don't have to get nasty. Just because you never take the time to put on makeup, that doesn't mean the rest of us don't care how we look."

Jessica made a face and moved in front of the mirror to brush her hair. "If that's your way of saying that some of us are not totally fixated on our appearance, I take it as a compliment."

Jessica brushed her hair with a few vigorous strokes. She didn't bother with makeup, but then she didn't need to. Her complexion glowed with health, and her green eyes were natural attention-getters.

Even Tara, who had retreated to the bench in front of her locker, had to admit that Jessica looked just fine. She was just feeling annoyed that Jessica had interrupted her when she was in the middle of her second favorite daydream. In her very favorite daydream she was a rock star, recording her first solo video. But that one required music.

And Tara especially needed her fantasies today. It was her eighteenth birthday, a big milestone in any girl's life, and so far not a single person had so much as wished her a happy birthday.

Of course, she hadn't told anyone at school that her birthday was coming up. But that was just the point. The average Tarenton High student probably thought of Tara Armstrong as one of the most popular girls in school. But popularity wasn't everything. Sure, she was a member of the cheerleading squad and had all the dates she wanted. In spite of that, she was often lonely. Other kids seemed to have special friends who found out about things like birthdays without being told. And who did she have?

This year, even her parents seemed content to let her birthday slip by. No doubt Marie, the Armstrongs' housekeeper, was baking a birthday cake for tonight's dessert. But her mother and father hadn't let so much as a hint slip about her birthday present.

Last fall, when she complained about having to take the bus to school, Dad had all but promised that she would be getting a car when she turned eighteen. Then, after Christmas, he suddenly dropped the subject. Had something happened to make him change his mind? Or had he just forgotten?

Out in the gym, Coach Ardith Engborg gave a shrill blast of her whistle, warning the stragglers that practice was about to begin. Tara jumped up and jogged out to join the others.

Olivia Evans, the squad captain, had already announced the first cheer. As soon as Tara took her place in line, Olivia raised her megaphone and began:

"Little Red Riding Hood,
Better watch out!
Our team is here to play!
Our team is here to shout!

Guess you know who we are,
We're the big . . . bad . . . WOLVES!!"

Petite, quiet Olivia was not the sort of person who would normally be out in front, leading the group. At the beginning of the year she had felt awkward about giving orders to the rest of the squad. Lately, though, she was getting better at her role.

As the squad ran through its repertoire of cheers, Olivia kept looking for ways it could improve. She noticed that Hope Chang needed to loosen up a little. Hope was the only junior on the squad, and her routines were always letter-perfect. The trouble was, Hope sometimes concentrated so hard on getting the moves right that she looked like a windup doll.

Olivia knew from experience what it was like to be the only junior on the squad. Criticizing Hope in front of the others would only make her more uptight.

"That was just about perfect," Olivia announced as the warmup ended. "Now, let's pair off and work on our tumbling. Hope, how about you working with me?"

Before Hope could answer, Olivia put an arm

around her shoulders and led her to the other side of the gym, where no one would overhear their conversation.

Jessica paired off with Sean Dubrow to practice high stags and T-lifts. Jessica was an excellent gymnast, and as Sean raised her into a T-lift, she kept her back straight and her toes pointed.

Sean, as usual, was having trouble keeping his mind on work. "You sure are an easy girl to pick up," he cracked as he lifted Jessica for the third time.

"All these lifts are easy if you do them right," she answered deadpan.

Tara stood nearby, pretending to do some stretches as she listened in on Jessica and Sean's conversation. Either Jessica honestly didn't realize Sean was flirting, or she was awfully good at ignoring the fact. Either way, it was a good joke on Sean. The more he flashed his toothpaste-ad smile and flexed his muscles, the more business-like Jessica became.

Tara looked around for Peter Rayman, who should have been paired off with her. Peter had excused himself to go out for a drink of water as soon as the warmup ended. That was over five minutes ago, and he hadn't come back yet.

Tara stopped pretending to exercise, and sat down on the mat. Hope and Olivia were over at the other side of the room, chatting about something they didn't want the others to hear. Sean was showing off. Peter had drifted off somewhere. She wasn't going to knock herself out working when the others were taking it easy.

* * *

Peter Rayman's mind was definitely not on practicing.

He was standing in front of the water fountain in the hall when he heard Betsey Dodson behind him, talking to another girl.

"Can you tell me where to find Mr. Engborg?" the girl asked Betsey.

"It's *Mrs.* Engborg," Betsey corrected her.

"Mr., Mrs., so what? How am I supposed to be able to tell? Ardith is some kind of hick name, either way."

Peter turned around, prepared to defend Coach Engborg, and found himself staring at a vision: long, sun-streaked blonde hair. Blue eyes. And a terrific figure, shown to advantage by a striped miniskirt and a pink, oversized sweat shirt that hung precariously off one shoulder.

On second glance, he realized that the girl must be wearing some sort of tank top underneath the sweat shirt. But that didn't alter the dramatic impression she made.

On third glance, he realized that she was staring at him.

"Maybe you can tell me where this Engborg person is," the girl suggested.

"Sure. She's in the gym. I'll show you the way. I mean, we wouldn't want you to get lost."

Betsey Dodson looked disgusted. "It's just down the hall. Who could get lost?"

Peter and the girl both ignored her, until she took the hint and walked away.

"I'm Diana," the girl said. "Diana Tucker. I

6

just transferred here from California. Santa Barbara, actually."

"I know."

"You do?"

Peter felt stupid. "I mean, I know you just transferred here," he explained. "Because if you'd been in school before today, I definitely would have noticed you."

"Oh, right."

Diana Tucker was so used to being noticed that it didn't occur to her to take this as a compliment. She accepted it as the obvious truth.

"Are you on the wrestling team or something?" she asked. "You really have a good build."

Peter felt his ears starting to tingle, the way they always did when he was embarrassed. He didn't have a lot of self-assurance when it came to terrific-looking girls, and now she was going to laugh at him when he told her the truth.

"Not exactly," he said. "I'm a cheerleader."

"Isn't that a coincidence! I was supposed to be a cheerleader this semester. But I found out that my family was moving, so I couldn't accept."

"That's too bad."

"This is the fifth time my folks have moved in four years. I've been in so many different schools I feel like an orphan. You probably don't know what that's like. I bet you have a zillion girl friends."

"Well, not exactly."

At the moment he only had one: Hope Chang. Just last week Hope had suggested that maybe they should each date other people. She liked him, but she was worried that they'd started going steady too soon. Peter had talked her out of the idea. Sometimes he thought he was crazy about Hope. At other times, he wondered if what he really wanted was security.

"I just don't know what I'm going to do with myself here," Diana was saying.

She sighed, pushing her lower lip out in an appealing pout. "My friends in California were so much more . . . sophisticated. This place is *nowhere* by comparison. I just know I'm going to be bored here."

"Oh, well. We find ways to amuse ourselves," Peter said defensively.

Diana smiled. "I bet. I'm sure you know how to keep a girl from getting bored."

Peter almost looked over his shoulder. Surely that remark couldn't have been meant for him! That was the kind of come-on that girls made to someone like Sean. Never to Peter Rayman.

CHAPTER

When Peter entered the gym with Diana, he saw that Coach Engborg had called the squad together to deliver a lecture. This was not good news. He must have been away from practice longer than he thought. His absence had definitely been noticed.

"I know you all had a good vacation in New Orleans," Mrs. Engborg was saying. "And that's great. But now you've got to get your minds back on practice."

Looks of guilt passed among the squad members.

"You started out fine today," their coach went on. "But as soon as you broke up to work in pairs, the practice fell apart. Sean started fooling around as usual. And I don't know what Olivia and Hope were so busy discussing. . . ."

9

Olivia felt her indignation rising. She had been talking to Hope about the importance of relaxing, about exchanging that frozen grin she sometimes wore for a genuine smile. Wasn't that as important as practicing tumbling runs and pyramids for the umpteenth time?

Hope spoke up in Olivia's defense. "We were talking about cheerleading, Coach. Honest. Livvy was helping me."

Coach Engborg was an understanding person most of the time, but she hated sloppiness and lack of discipline. And once she started lecturing on her favorite subject, she had no intention of letting herself be interrupted.

"Fine," she snapped, brushing aside Hope's explanation. "But Olivia is the captain. She should have noticed that the others were goofing off."

"Whew!" Diana said under her breath to Peter. "Talk about a dictator!"

Peter shook his head. "Coach isn't so bad."

Fortunately, Coach Engborg hadn't heard Diana's remark. But she did hear Peter.

She scowled. "Thank you for that vote of confidence, Mr. Rayman. Since you think so, maybe you won't mind sticking around for practice next time, instead of wandering off."

It was bad enough to be told off by the coach, even though Peter knew he probably deserved it. But he hated to be talked to like a bad boy in front of Diana. "I was just getting a drink of water," he said defiantly.

Coach Engborg looked at Diana and raised an

eyebrow in disbelief. Tara giggled.

"I guess that's enough said for now," the coach said. "Let's try to do better next time."

As the practice broke up, Diana waved her program card and she and Ardith Engborg disappeared into the coach's office.

Sean Dubrow's eyes were practically falling out of his head. "Who is *that*?" he demanded of Peter. "What a fox! You don't see a figure like that very often!"

"She's just some transfer student," Peter mumbled. Sometimes Sean really ticked him off. You could already see the little wheels turning inside his brain. He seemed to assume that every good-looking girl who came into sight was going to fall for him sooner or later. And usually he was right.

Sean, oblivious to Peter's thoughts, clapped him on the shoulder. "Well, I don't blame you for cutting practice, old boy. Who can concentrate on cheerleading when heaven is so near?"

This was too much for Hope. "Why don't you grow up?" she asked Sean accusingly. "Don't you think we get tired of hearing these reports on the state of your hormones all the time?"

"You said it!" agreed Jessica.

Sean didn't look the least bit embarrassed. "Some of us are brainy. Some of us just have healthy hormones. Can I help it?"

Sean walked toward the boys' locker room, whistling happily.

"Sometimes he makes me so mad," Hope said.

11

"You'd think he never saw a female before. I mean, what are *we*? How can he be so interested in some girl he's never even talked to? For all he knows, she's not even a nice person."

"Uh huh," said Peter. Sometimes he wished Hope weren't so logical.

Hope took his hand. "I'm just glad you aren't like Sean," she said. "You're so . . . steady."

Peter wanted to gag. Was that the best compliment Hope could come up with? He didn't want to change places with Sean. Not permanently, anyway. But it certainly would be interesting to know what it was like to have girls hanging all over him, just once in his life.

Inside the coach's office, Diana was not very pleased with the way the discussion was going.

"None of these phys. ed. classes sound very interesting," she said. "I was on the golf team at my last school. I don't suppose you even have a golf team here."

"Well, no." Coach Engborg smiled. "It's a little difficult to play golf in the snow, and we have a lot of it."

Diana made a face. "Snow is so boring. It ruins everything."

Coach Engborg was beginning to get impatient. "There's nothing I can do about the snow. You'll just have to get used to it."

"I used to be on the tennis team, too," Diana went on. "I don't suppose you have one of those, either."

12

"No, we don't. How about basketball? You have the height for it."

Diana seemed insulted. "I don't care for team sports. All that junk about cooperating for the good of the team really turns me off. I'm an individualist."

"I see." Coach Engborg looked unimpressed. "In that case, let's sign you up for swimming. Since you're from California, you must know how to swim."

"No way." Diana shook her head. "I'm not going to expose my hair to all that chlorine. I'm used to swimming in the ocean. Or at least in outdoor pools. Swimming indoors is creepy."

"I give up." Coach Engborg took Diana's program card and held her ballpoint pen poised above it in midair. "You tell me what sport you want to sign up for."

"I was thinking that I might like to be a cheerleader."

The coach's mouth dropped open in surprise. "I thought you didn't like team sports. Team spirit is what cheerleading is all about."

Diana pouted. "That's different. Cheerleaders are . . . well, leaders."

"I see you're only a junior," the coach said, glancing at Diana's program card. "You're certainly welcome to try out this June with everyone else. But in the meantime, you have to take physical education."

"I don't think that's fair," Diana protested. "I wasn't here last year when tryouts were held. Why

13

shouldn't I have my chance to make the squad? Can't you hold a special tryout for me now?"

"No, I can't. You'll have to wait until June. In any case, there are no vacancies on the squad."

No was not a word that Diana Tucker was used to hearing very often. She usually managed to get her way.

"Won't you give me a chance?" she wheedled. "I know all the moves. And I look like a cheerleader. I'm certainly more of a natural leader than that little mouse Olivia What's-her-name."

Coach Engborg frowned. "Olivia may not be a natural leader, but she's earned her job. No one I've ever coached has worked harder. She's excellent. And if you put in just half the effort she has, you might have a chance of being a Varsity Cheerleader someday yourself."

The coach's pen made a decisive check beside one of the empty squares on Diana's program card. "As for now, you are hereby assigned to intramural basketball. Maybe it will teach you a little something about the spirit of cooperation.

Diana flipped her sun-streaked blonde hair in a gesture of sulky resentment and strode out of the coach's office without answering.

Out in the parking lot, she located her car, a trim white Volkswagen Jetta. She'd chosen the color back in California, with visions of driving along the coastal highway on a sunny day. Now the little car's doors and fenders were streaked with dirt, and she realized that white was the worst possible color for a northern climate.

Angrily, she jerked open the front door and threw her books inside.

"Hey, nice car!"

Diana looked up and saw Betsey Dodson getting into the car parked next to hers.

"It was a nice car until it got all this filth on it," she snapped and hopped into the car, slamming the door shut behind her.

Betsey had been assigned by the principal's office to make sure that Diana found her way around during her first day at Tarenton High. Although she was a little bit hurt that Diana hadn't been more friendly, she'd been trying to be a good sport. But being nice to Diana was turning out to be a losing proposition.

Betsey turned to her friend Sally Cook. "Can you believe that? That girl is really something. You should have seen the way she was playing up to Peter Rayman today."

"Oh, well," said Sally, "Peter is too sensible to be taken in by Miss California's act."

Betsey looked uncertain. "I'm not sure about that. What I can't figure out is why Diana seemed so interested in Peter. Of course he's really nice, but I think Sean is more her type."

Sally shrugged. "Maybe she's just like that with every guy she meets. Diana doesn't strike me as the type who thinks ahead."

But Sally was wrong on that score. As she drove home from her first day at Tarenton High, Diana was already working on a plan.

It hadn't taken her long to figure out that cheerleading was a big deal at Tarenton. She'd seen the trophies in the case in the front hall and heard kids talking at lunch about some pep rally that was coming up. Being a cheerleader would certainly make her life less boring for the next few months.

And Coach Engborg had given her an idea. The coach said she couldn't hold a midyear tryout because there weren't any vacancies on the squad. But what if there *was* a vacancy?

Diana smiled to herself. When there was something she really, really wanted, she could work as hard as anyone to get it. She just preferred to use her own methods. With a little work, she should have no trouble thinking up a scheme that would get one of the cheerleaders off the squad.

CHAPTER

The first thing Tara noticed when she got home from practice was the covered cake plate sitting on the kitchen counter, half-hidden behind the Cuisinart. Carefully, she lifted the lid and took a peek at Marie's handiwork: a home-decorated birthday cake that any bakery would be proud to sell. Marie had even remembered to use mocha-flavored frosting, her favorite. Tara smiled to herself. At least one person hadn't forgotten her birthday!

Her mother was in the living room, playing bridge with three members of her club, as usual. A pall of smoke hung over the table.

"I just don't understand why you bid three diamonds, Cecelia," Mrs. Armstrong was saying to her partner.

Tara sighed. Playing bridge wasn't so bad, but

she could never understand how her mother and her friends could spend hours rehashing a game that was already over and done with. Talk about boring!

"Is that you, Tara?" her mother called out. "We're having dinner at six-thirty. I hope you have a good appetite. Marie insisted on making a wickedly rich cake. I don't know why birthdays can't be celebrated in some way that isn't fattening."

Tara tried to think of the possibilities. Maybe birthday Jell-O, except that the candles would probably sink into the Jell-O and snuff themselves out. Normally, the mental picture might have been funny. But why did her mom have to turn everything, even her birthday, into something to complain about?

By the time dinnertime rolled around, Tara had forgotten about her anger. Marie had made roast chicken with herb dressing, one of her favorite meals. And her dad had a pleased look on his face that made her sure that her birthday present hadn't been completely forgotten.

Sure enough, as soon as Tara had blown out the candles on her cake, her dad slipped into his study and returned with a box wrapped in silver paper.

Well, it certainly isn't a car, Tara told herself. Judging from the size of the box, it looked more like a pair of shoes.

Tara unwrapped the silver foil carefully, revealing an oblong music box with a handpainted picture of a ballerina on the cover. When the lid was opened, the box played "Dance of the Hours."

She knew that the music box was a valuable antique. It had once belonged to her grandmother Mamie, and her great-grandmother before that. Her mother kept it wrapped in tissue paper in the cedar chest in her room.

"I came across that box the other day," Mrs. Armstrong explained, "and I couldn't help thinking what a shame it was to keep it stored away out of sight. I know Mamie would have wanted you to have it. And, well, I do, too."

Tara felt her anger against her mother melting. "Thanks, Mom," she said, "It's beautiful."

Of course, it wasn't exactly the present she'd been hoping for. But she did her best not to let her disappointment show.

Across the table, her dad cleared his throat loudly. "I think if you look, you'll find an envelope taped to the bottom of the box."

Tara turned the box over and found it: a tiny white envelope about two inches by two inches. Inside, she found a key. But what was it? The key to the music box?

No. It looked more like a car key!

Tara looked at her father in amazement. He beamed back at her. "I see for once we managed to surprise you," he said. "It's out in the driveway. Go take a look."

"Daddy! You're fantastic! You're both fantastic!" Tara threw her arms around her father and gave him a big hug, then bolted for the door.

Parked in the driveway was a gold-colored Chevy convertible. She could hardly believe it!

"Of course it isn't new," her father said when she'd finished screeching for joy. "It's four years old, and has quite a few miles on it. It belonged to one of the associates in my law office, so I got a very good deal."

"I only agreed," put in Mrs. Armstrong, "because it isn't really fair to ask Marie to play chauffeur for an eighteen-year-old."

"That's right," said her dad, "A car is a big responsibility. I certainly hope you're ready to take it on."

Tara was so ecstatic that for once she didn't let her parents' dire warnings get her down. She was a good driver — better than her mother. And what did her folks think she was going to do, anyway? Take the car and run away from home? Take up drag racing?

"Can I take it out tonight?" she asked as soon as the warnings were over with. "Just to try it out?"

"I don't see why not," said Mr. Armstrong. "It is your car, after all."

Her mother insisted that Tara help her stack the dishes and run the dishwasher first. Since Marie had baked a cake, which she didn't have to do, it wasn't fair that she find the dirty dishes waiting for her when she arrived the next morning.

But as soon as the chore was finished, Tara jumped into the front seat of the Chevy and very carefully put it into gear. She could still hardly believe it was true. Her own car! Now she wouldn't have to depend on the bus anymore. Or on getting rides with other kids from school. She was free to go anywhere she wanted!

The first thing she wanted to do was to find some of her friends and show off her wonderful present. She drove slowly through Tarenton, past The Pancake House on Main Street, looking for familiar cars. Next she checked out the Pizza Palace and the mall. Where was everybody? Home studying?

Since no one she knew seemed to be in any of the obvious hangouts, she even tried driving past Sean Dubrow's house. But his red Fiero wasn't in the driveway.

She drove by Hope Chang's house, but Mrs. Chang said that Hope had talked Peter into taking her to a concert at the junior college in Hillsborough.

At the Bennetts', Jessica's stepfather came to the door and said that Jessica and her mother had gone to visit a relative.

Tara was beginning to feel frustrated. Part of the fun of having a car was sharing it with your friends. But where were her friends?

Driving aimlessly, she found herself headed down the street where Olivia Evans lived. At least there was someone at home there. The Evans' house was brightly lit.

She pulled into the driveway and headed for the Evans' front door. Olivia, who'd been doing her math homework in the kitchen, saw her coming and opened the door after one knock.

"Hi" said Tara brightly. "Guess what? I got a car for my birthday."

"That's *terrific!*"

Olivia followed Tara outside to admire the car. Some girls had all the luck! Tara had been lucky enough to be born with gorgeous red hair. She had a figure that would stop traffic, too. And now her parents had just handed her the keys to a car. She hadn't even had to work for it.

"I'm lucky my mother even lets me go out of the house alone," Olivia said enviously. "I'll probably be thirty years old before she thinks I'm ready to have my own car."

Tara laughed. "Would you like to come for a drive?" she asked. "You can be my first passenger."

"Sure. I'd love to."

As she ran inside to get her coat and tell her parents where she was going, Olivia couldn't help wondering why Tara had picked her to invite. Of the three other girls on the squad, she had the least in common with Tara. They probably would never have spoken to each other if they didn't both happen to be cheerleaders.

As they drove away from the Evans' house, Tara obviously didn't know where to go next. "I've already been around town," she told Olivia. "There's no one around. It's deader than usual."

Olivia was beginning to understand why Tara had come to see her. She was the last resort.

"How about driving over to Dopey's?" she suggested, swallowing her pride.

"That's a great idea!"

Dopey's was a hamburger and barbecue place on the road just west of town. Tara had always thought that it was the customers who should be called "dopey" for going there. The food certainly wasn't very good. But Dopey's did a lot of takeout business, so it was a good place to hang around if you wanted to see people.

And tonight was no exception. When they pulled into the parking lot, they noticed a very familiar car in the space next to them — Pres Tilford's red Porsche.

Olivia brightened immediately. She still felt closer to Pres Tilford and some of the other graduates of last year's squad than she did to her own classmates.

She led Tara inside and scanned the crowd for Pres's familiar face. Almost immediately, she spotted him in one of the rear booths. With him was a tall, slim blonde who looked from a distance like Mary Ellen Kirkwood.

Olivia pushed her way through the crowd by the takeout counter, with Tara close behind. "Mary Ellen," she said. "What are you doing in town? I thought you were in New York."

The blonde turned around and gave Olivia a chilly look. She certainly wasn't Mary Ellen. And she didn't look very friendly, either.

"Have you met Diana Tucker?" Pres asked, none too pleased at Olivia's mistake.

"Oh, I'm sorry," Olivia apologized. "You're the girl who was in the gym this afternoon, right? I hope you got your schedule fixed up the way you wanted it."

"Not exactly," Diana said. "I was just telling Preston, here, how disappointed I am to be stuck taking intramural sports. At my last school, in Santa Barbara, I was captain of the cheerleading squad. Of course, we didn't wear those old-fashioned uniforms that you have here in Tarenton. Pleated skirts and sweaters! I mean, how quaint can you get?"

"What *did* you wear?" Tara asked eagerly.

"Metallic-gold spandex body suits," said Diana. "And when it was too warm for those, we had halter tops and short shorts."

Pres looked skeptical. "I don't think Tarenton is quite ready for that look," he said. "And I know Coach Engborg isn't ready for it."

"I don't know about that," Diana said. "The coach was very interested to hear my ideas."

"She was?" Olivia said suspiciously. She didn't like the way this conversation was going at all.

"Of course, it's really up to the squad captain to set the tone," Diana went on. She looked straight at Olivia. "The coach was sorry she picked on you at practice. Actually, she said some nice things about you to me."

"Like what?" Olivia demanded.

Diana examined her long pink nails. "Well, she said you've been trying hard, even though you don't *really* have what it takes to be a natural leader."

"I don't believe it!" Olivia shot back.

Diana put a hand in front of her mouth. "Oh, I'm sorry! I guess I shouldn't have told you that. But Ardith — I mean, Coach Engborg — meant it to be kind. Of course, she also said that she wouldn't consider making any changes in the squad without holding a tryout first. I mean, when the time comes."

Olivia's mouth had dropped open in shock.

Diana began studying the oversized sports watch that she wore on her left arm. Olivia noticed that it was pink, matching her designer sweat shirt. This girl probably had a different watch to go with every outfit in her closet.

"Well, I've got to be running along," Diana announced, standing to go. "I do an hour and a half of exercises every evening. Some of us have to work hard if we want to keep our figures." This remark was delivered with a pointed glance in Tara's direction. "You know what I mean, don't you Tara?" Diana added for good measure. "You look like the type who has to worry about all those extra desserts going straight to your hips."

On that note, Diana departed.

Tara made a face. "Something tells me that Diana Tucker and I are not going to get along," she predicted.

"Don't let her bother you," Pres said. "There is absolutely nothing wrong with your hips."

"Believe me, I'm not worried," Tara assured him. "But if the letter 'I' ever gets cut out of the alphabet, Diana is going to be in big trouble. She's the most self-centered person I've ever met."

25

Pres laughed. "Coming from you, Tara, that's quite a statement."

Tara pushed her hair off her forehead. "Okay, I admit it. I'm a little bit conceited sometimes. But I'm in the minor leagues compared to her."

Olivia was still in shock. "Will you stop arguing about who's the most conceited. Didn't you hear what she said? Coach Engborg is talking about holding another tryout and replacing me as captain!"

"I don't believe it," said Pres. "She would never say that."

"You're right," agreed Tara. "Why would she?"

"But why would Diana make up a story like that?" Olivia wondered.

Pres shrugged. "Who knows?"

"Well, I'm not going to just forget it," Olivia vowed. "If the coach has doubts about me, I'm going to make sure I find out and do something about them."

The girls said good-bye to Pres and headed back out to the Chevy. They stepped outside just in time to see Diana's little white car pulling out onto the highway at top speed.

Even though she didn't like Diana, Tara felt that she understood her. It couldn't be easy being the new girl in town. Diana was just trying to one-up everyone before they had a chance to do the same thing to her. It was much harder for Tara to understand someone like Olivia. Livvy was so sincere that sometimes she practically asked to be bullied.

As they drove home in silence, Tara wondered just how far Diana would go to get her way. It didn't worry her very much one way or the other. Because one thing she knew for sure: She was too smart to ever let Diana get the better of her.

CHAPTER

"I hate away games," said Hope as the squad climbed aboard the minibus for the trip to Grove Lake. "It's so much more fun cheering in front of the home crowd."

"I wouldn't worry about tonight's game," said Sean. "The Pompon Squad had so many kids signed up for the game that they had to charter a second bus. You've got to give Holly Hudson credit. A lot of people don't want to put in any effort on behalf of school spirit if they can't be out front leading cheers. But Holly has really worked hard since she was elected president of the Pompon Squad."

"I heard Holly's been talking about having the squad members wear matching red and white sweaters," Tara said. "I think it's a good idea.

That way they would really be noticed, even at away games."

An hour or so later, when the game got underway in the Grove Lake gymnasium, the cheerleaders found out about another of Holly's great ideas. The Pompon Squad had been practicing card stunts all week long, and each member had come to the game equipped with a set of huge flash cards.

When the game started, Holly stood in front of the visitors' section, calling out cues for the various stunts. She was wearing a dark red sweater with a wolf's head symbol on the front, red slacks, and white legwarmers. With her dark hair cut in a spiky modified punk style, and dangly silver earrings in her ears, she made a riveting sight.

When Holly called out the signal for stunt number one, the entire Pompon Squad section dived for their cards and held them overhead, spelling out the phrase GO WOLVES.

The signal for stunt number two produced the call for DEE-FENSE!!!

Stunt number three was a picture of Tarenton's wolf head logo.

And stunt number four, for use when the other team missed a basket, read OOPS!!

When Holly first thought about doing card stunts, the plan had been to do one or two stunts during halftime. Then Diana Tucker had come up with the idea of using words that could be keyed to what was going on during the game.

"We did it back in California," Diana had

said. "Of course, it might be too complicated for you to work out."

That had been all Holly needed to hear. She could never walk away from a challenge. Now she was proud that she'd managed to organize the stunts in just one week. That would show Diana that there was nothing second-best about Tarenton.

Time after time, during the first half of the game, Olivia called for a cheer only to find that no one in the bleachers was paying attention. The Pompon Squad section was watching Holly for their next cue. Or worse yet, they had their heads hidden behind those big flash cards.

Olivia couldn't decide what to do. She wanted to march right over to Holly and tell her to cut it out. But what if she refused? She didn't want to get involved in an argument right there in front of the crowd, especially if the Pompon Squad was going to take Holly's side. If Mary Ellen was still captain, Olivia thought, she would know exactly how to handle this.

When halftime came, at long last, Olivia was so distracted that she could hardly concentrate on the routine. The squad had practiced a new pyramid that they were planning to use at that night's game for the first time. Hope sat on Tara's shoulders. Then Olivia, while doing a split, was lifted up by Sean and Peter. When she was high enough in the air, she was able to rest her arms on Hope's shoulders. Jessica was the spotter.

The pyramid had worked fine in practice. But today, just as they got started, Olivia noticed that

Holly was calling for yet another card stunt. She was so angry that she forgot to hold herself steady in the split. Peter made a quick adjustment to keep from dropping her. He managed, but in the meantime she lost her balance completely. She ended up hanging upside down.

Making a quick recovery, she did a forward roll, jumped up, and continued with the next part of the routine. But the awkward mistake had been noticed. Holly gave a signal and the Pompon Squad raised the cards that spelled out OOPS!! The stadium erupted in laughter.

That did it! As soon as the routine was finished, Olivia made her way to the sidelines and confronted Holly. "You're supposed to be cooperating with the cheerleaders, not making us look dumb!" she yelled. "What's the big idea?"

"But it was just a joke," pleaded Holly. "Don't you have a sense of humor?"

"A sense of humor! You've been doing everything possible to compete with us all evening long. I want you to cut it out right now!"

Holly turned angrily toward the Pompon Squad. "Sorry group. The cheerleaders didn't like our contribution. We have been officially requested to stop."

There were a few scattered boo's from the rear of the Pompon section. No one looked very happy.

Olivia stalked away, trying to tell herself that she'd won the argument. But it sure didn't feel like a victory.

On the bus trip home, no one had much to say.

Olivia was in no mood to hear Coach Engborg's views on the card stunt incident, and the coach didn't volunteer an opinion. The rest of the squad could see that Olivia was still steaming, so they decided to drop the subject for the time being.

When the minibus reached the Tarenton High parking lot, Olivia immediately left the group to join her boyfriend, David Duffy, who was waiting for her in his car. Duffy was a sports reporter for the *Tarenton Lighter*, so he'd been at the game and witnessed the entire disaster at halftime.

"Don't say a word," Olivia warned as she took her place in the front seat beside him. "I don't want sympathy right now."

"Okay," Duffy agreed. "Never let it be said that I'm uncooperative."

Sometimes Duffy's lean, angular face was like a mask. Olivia could never tell whether he was kidding or not. "Is that your way of telling me that the verdict is pretty bad?"

"Well, since you insist on knowing — "

Olivia interrupted him. "I know I must've looked dumb, hanging upside down like that."

"Oh, that." Duffy waved the idea away. "No one cares about that. You've got to risk making a mistake once in a while if you're going to try new routines. Besides, I thought you looked kind of cute flopping around out there."

"Duffy! Be serious!"

"Okay. Seriously speaking, I thought you handled it all wrong tonight. You didn't object to the card stunts as long as they were just distracting attention from the game. Then, as soon as the joke was on you, you were full of righteous indignation."

Olivia realized right away that Duffy was right. She hadn't been thinking about the game at all, only about how Holly was upstaging the cheerleaders.

"How am I ever going to get this straightened out?" she wondered aloud.

"I guess you'll have to have a talk with Holly," Duffy suggested. "But for tonight, let's just forget about it. Anyway, the evening wasn't a total loss. I got a terrific photo of you in midflop. It's going to be on the front page of the next issue of the *Tarenton Lighter*."

"You didn't!"

"I did, too. The magic camera of David Duffy sees all."

Fortunately, Duffy had this secret dimple on his chin that only made an appearance when he was teasing. It was visible now, despite Duffy's best efforts to control it.

"You rat! You didn't really." She reached over quickly and gave him a little pinch.

"Hey, don't do that! You know I'm ticklish."

"Of course I know it."

They had pulled into the Evans' driveway and come to a stop just beyond the reach of the nearest streetlight. "Okay, I confess. I was just kidding. But now, let's try a serious experiment."

"Like what?"

"Let's see how long we can sit here kissing before your mother starts blinking the porch lights on and off."

"Knowing my mother, I'd say about two minutes. She's probably watching us right now from her bedroom window. I bet she's been stationed there all evening, waiting for me to come home."

Duffy immediately rolled down his window, leaned out, and waved in the direction of Mrs. Evans' bedroom. "Hi there, Mrs. Evans. We're home. You can relax now," he called out.

Sure enough, Olivia saw a shadow moving behind the bedroom drapes. Then, to her surprise, Mrs. Evans peeked out from behind the drapes and waved back. It was impossible to hear what she was saying through the closed windows, but they saw her smile a bit guiltily and mouth the words, "Hello, Duffy."

"I can hardly believe it," said Olivia, "but I think my mother likes you."

"Why? Am I so unlikable?"

"No, but my mother automatically regards any boy I go out with as the enemy. She's pretty much of a dragon."

"I don't know about that. I think your mother's kind of cute. More like a mother hen fussing over her little chick."

Olivia stared at Duffy, her brown eyes wide. It was the first time she had ever heard her mother described as cute. "Either you're completely crazy," she gasped, "or else — "

Duffy grinned. "Or else, what?"

She had been going to say, "Or else you're in love with me." But she had stopped herself just in time. Duffy wasn't serious about anything, so how could he be in love? And even if he was, she wasn't sure how she would feel about it.

"Forget it," she said. "Let's get back to that experiment you were talking about."

"I thought you'd never ask," Duffy joked. But as he pulled her close to him, Olivia noticed that the "teasing" dimple on his chin had completely disappeared.

As soon as Olivia left the group, Tara had volunteered to take the other cheerleaders out for an after-game snack. Everyone piled into the Chevy except for Sean, who followed behind in his red Fiero.

"How about The Pancake House?" suggested Jessica from her place in the backseat. She hoped that her voice sounded casual. She didn't want the group to suspect that she had an ulterior motive for wanting to go there, but The Pancake House happened to be where Patrick Henley often stopped for a meal after working late.

Jessica hadn't seen much of Patrick since they returned from the semester break trip to New Orleans. He was putting in long hours with H&T's TLC Moving, the company he had started with Pres Tilford. With her at school during the day, and Patrick working so many evenings and weekends, their romance sometimes seemed doomed.

When they pulled into The Pancake House parking lot, Jessica immediately spotted the H&T moving van. So did Peter, who announced, "Look who's here. No wonder Jessica had a sudden craving for Pancake House food!"

Inside the restaurant, Patrick was sitting at one of the single tables near the counter, rereading a letter he'd received earlier in the day.

Dear Patrick, it began:

I thought I should write to tell you that I'm probably coming back to Tarenton in a month or so for a visit. New York is fine, even though I'm not exactly taking the fashion world by storm. But I miss Tarenton a lot more than I expected to. It's hard being in a big city where you don't have any real friends. There are days when I enjoy it, but there are lots of lonely times, too.

Here's the part of my news that I don't quite know how to tell you. You probably know that I've been writing to Pres since my last visit. Well, he's part of the reason I'm thinking about coming back to Tarenton. It's too early to tell for sure, but I think Pres and I may be starting to get seriously involved. That's kind of funny, isn't it, considering that I could never get Pres's total attention when we were on the squad together and saw each other practically every day?

I hear you're going out with Jessica Bennett now, so I hope this is all right with you. Of course, I want us to stay good friends.

Love,
Mary Ellen

Patrick had read the letter at least a dozen times since he received it. Every time, he waited for his heart to stop beating, but that never quite happened. Not that he was wildly enthusiastic about the prospect of Mary Ellen coming back to Tarenton as Pres's girl friend. For months he had expected that somehow, some way, he and Mary Ellen would end up together. She was his first love, and giving up on her was like saying good-bye to an important part of his life.

But he didn't mind as much as he felt he should. Amazingly, he wasn't hung up on Mary Ellen anymore. At least not more than a little bit. Jessica was fast taking Mary Ellen's place. For one thing, it was great to have a girl friend who wasn't ashamed of him for doing hard, manual labor. Jessica wasn't ashamed of being seen in his truck, either.

The more he thought about it, he could hardly imagine why he ever thought he and Mary Ellen could work out their differences. . . .

"Patrick! Are you all right?"

Patrick looked up from his thoughts and saw Jessica standing at his table with the other cheerleaders. He realized that his meal was sitting cold and untouched in front of him. He'd been in a complete daze.

"Hi, Jessica. Sure I'm all right. Just tired I guess," he said.

He moved to join Jessica and the others in a booth, staying long enough to get a full report on the squad's problems with Holly Hudson, and the new girl, Diana Tucker. Then he and Jessica left together.

"I wish Tara hadn't gotten so carried away on the subject of Diana," Jessica said, as soon as they were alone together. "Did you see the look on Peter's face? I think he actually likes Diana.

"But," Jessica added, "you can't help wondering if there's anything to that part about the coach losing faith in Olivia. Do you suppose she's seriously thinking about replacing Livvy as captain?"

"Of course not," Patrick snorted. "Diana is a troublemaker from the word go. In fact, she reminds me a lot of Vanessa Barlow. You didn't have too many dealings with Vanessa because you were only a junior last year. But believe me, they're the same type. Beautiful but deadly."

Jessica didn't like the look that came into Patrick's blue eyes sometimes when he talked about his experiences with other girls even though she knew he'd never liked Vanessa. She had dated a lot of different guys before Patrick. but he was the first one she had ever really cared about. She liked his large body and his rugged smile and the way he moved, powerful and graceful at the same time. Even little things about him. like the way he rolled up the sleeves of his T-shirt over his muscular arms appealed to her. Patrick was the first boyfriend she'd ever cared enough about to feel jealous of his old flames.

Of course, the memory that bothered her most was of Mary Ellen Kirkwood. Patrick's pursuit of Mary Ellen was legendary. She wondered if he would ever care half as much about her.

Patrick was still on memory lane. "Vanessa was really something," he said. "She almost had her claws into me a few times, I admit."

"Will you stop it!" Jessica said, annoyed. "Don't you think I get tired of being reminded that you're such an expert on women? First Mary Ellen. Now Vanessa."

"Who said anything about Mary Ellen?"

"No one. I just get the feeling that Mary Ellen's ghost is always around. Especially in this truck."

Patrick chuckled. "Mary Ellen would hate to hear that. First of all, she's very much alive. So she doesn't have a ghost. And if she did, you can be sure that this truck is the last place it would choose to haunt. Mary Ellen was not the truck type."

"And I am?"

Patrick's hands tensed on the steering wheel. "Honestly, Jessica, my crush on Mary Ellen is history. Over and done with."

Jess wanted to believe it, but she was still suspicious. "Really? And you haven't been writing to her and not mentioning it?"

Patrick thought of the letter that was burning a hole in his pocket that very minute. It was hardly a love letter. In fact, he'd been hoping to find a way to tell Jessica about Mary Ellen and Pres, and about his discovery that he didn't even feel jealous anymore.

But on second thought, the letter wouldn't exactly help his case. That Mary Ellen was interested in someone else was no great news. If anything, the letter made it clear that Mary Ellen thought he still cared about her.

Patrick decided to be diplomatic for once. In other words, he was going to lie. "Of course not," he assured Jessica. "Of course we're not writing to each other."

"That's good," said Jessica. "Because I don't think I could stand it if I found out you were lying."

CHAPTER

5

Diana Tucker had spent a good part of her weekend shopping for clothes.

On Monday morning, she showed up at school wearing a dyed fake-rabbit jacket in a grayish-lavender shade known as Heather Haze. Her feet and calves were encased in gray lizard-look boots. Underneath her jacket, she was wearing a lavender cashmere sweater with an off-center scoop neck that showed a good deal of her sun-tanned upper back. Her mini had been exchanged for a midcalf wool skirt that made up for its length by sporting a dramatic slit on one side.

Tara, Hope, and Peter happened to be standing in the front lobby when Diana made her big entrance. Hope took one look at Diana and shook her head. "How can anyone come to school so overdressed?" she asked.

"That isn't quite the word I'd use," Tara said. "For some reason, Diana always looks to me as if her clothes are about to fall off any second."

Peter had had exactly the same thought. But hearing it from Tara, he didn't like it. "Give her a break," he said.

"Why should I?" said Tara.

"Because it's obvious that you're just jealous."

"I am not!" Tara pulled her wool coat closer around her neck and stalked away in a huff.

"That wasn't a very nice thing to say," Hope chided him, as soon as Tara was out of earshot.

"Nice!" Peter groused. "There's that word again! Why am I always supposed to be the nice one? Nice, easy-going Peter, that's me. That's what everyone thinks, isn't it?"

Hope was startled. "Well, what's wrong with that?"

Peter couldn't think of an answer that didn't sound dumb. "Look," he said, "Let's not start an argument, okay?"

"I'm not starting an argument," Hope insisted. "I'm just trying to figure out what the problem is."

"There's no problem. And don't keep after me to explain every single remark I make. Just forget it!"

Peter headed for his homeroom, leaving Hope staring at his departing back. What had she done?

Hope hadn't meant to nag. But Peter's strong reaction made her feel that she must be at fault. Lately, she felt half afraid to say *anything* around Peter. She just couldn't seem to please him. Maybe girls like Diana had the right idea after

42

all, she told herself. It didn't pay to act natural. If only she could just learn to keep her mouth shut and rely on that helpless, little girl pout that Diana used to get her way!

While Hope brooded through her morning classes, Diana's day was off to a busy start.

Her first class was girls' basketball, taught by Mrs. Engborg. There was nothing that Diana hated more than running around the gym with a bunch of other girls, getting all sweaty and ruining her hairdo, which she'd worked so hard on that morning. As long as Mrs. Engborg was at the other end of the court, working on drills with another group, Diana lounged near the wall, passing up her turn to practice dribbling and shooting as many times as she could get away with. But when she noticed the coach coming down court, she quickly cut into the line, grabbed the next rebound, and moved in for a jump shot.

Thwump! The ball slipped through the hoop.

The girl who was supposed to be guarding was so stunned by Diana's shooting out of turn that she never even raised her arms. And the girl who had been cut off just stood there, giving Diana a dirty look and ignoring her chance to get the rebound.

Mrs. Engborg, watching the action from a distance, didn't catch what was going on. "Nice shot," she yelled to Diana. "The rest of you, look lively. Don't just stand there. Your feet will grow roots."

Later, when the coach called for a passing

drill, the other girls tried to get back at Diana by freezing her out, refusing to pass her the ball. Naturally, this time Coach Engborg noticed exactly what was going on.

"What's wrong with this group today?" she asked. "Stop hogging the ball and let the new girl play."

Diana looked the picture of innocence while the other girls in her drill group gritted their teeth and shunted the ball her way.

When the class ended, Diana made sure she latched on to Holly Hudson. Holly had been part of another drill section, so she hadn't noticed Diana's antics. "How do you like it here, so far?" Holly asked, as they headed for the locker room.

Diana shrugged. "What's to like? In my old school, we had coed gym. You could take golf, tennis . . . even windsurfing."

"No kidding!" Holly was impressed. "You're so lucky. I mean, you *were* so lucky. I guess Tarenton High is a big comedown for you."

Diana didn't deny it. "Don't you just hate it that they make you take this course?" she said.

Holly thought this over. She was a small girl with a big voice, who had taken modern dance and dramatics since she was in grade school. She thought of herself as an extrovert, but a lot of other people thought she was just plain pushy, always looking to be the center of attention. "Not really." she admitted. "This is the only class I have where the teacher isn't always telling me to be quiet."

"By the way, how did those card stunts work out?" Diana asked.

"Not so well. Olivia and the rest of the cheerleaders didn't exactly appreciate them."

"I bet she's just afraid that when Coach Engborg dumps her that you'll end up getting her place on the squad."

"Dumps her! Who said the coach is going to dump Olivia?"

Diana pretended to clamp her lips shut. "Oh dear! I guess I wasn't supposed to mention it."

"Mention what? You can tell me!" Holly was almost green with curiosity.

"Well, it's just something the coach let slip when I talked to her about signing my program card," Diana whispered. "She hinted that she's very unhappy with Olivia. She even said there might be a midyear tryout to fill a vacancy on the squad."

Holly's dark eyes grew wide. "No kidding!"

"I'm sure all the new ideas you have for the Pompon Squad are making a big impression on the coach," Diana told her. "I heard you're even going to get sweaters."

"Right. I thought maybe we should all get matching sweaters in the school colors."

"You should have seen the uniforms the Pompon Squad had back at my old school," Diana rolled her eyes. "We had shirts, of course. But we had jackets, too. Nothing cheap, either. They were aviator style, with padded shoulders and gussets in front, and lined with real silk. I bet

45

you could design something like that in Tarenton's colors."

Diana paused, as if some new thought had just occurred to her. "Of course, you'd never get the other kids to go along. Nobody around here is much interested in new ideas. Except you, of course."

Holly felt insulted on Tarenton's behalf. "That's not true. If it can be done in California, it can be done here. I'll tell you what . . . the Pompon Squad is having a steering committee meeting in the cafeteria at lunchtime. Why don't you sit in and we'll talk about the idea?"

The steering committee didn't look too happy about having Diana sit in on their meeting, but they listened patiently as she described the style of jackets she had in mind.

"Diana and I would do the actual designing," Holly put in excitedly. "And then I'm sure we could order them through Marnie's. The owner, Mrs. Gunderson, would know some company that could run them up for us pretty quickly."

"How much are these jackets going to cost?" asked Carla Simpson, the squad's secretary.

"Gee, I hadn't thought about that." Holly looked at Diana for help.

Diana flipped her blonde hair in annoyance, silently communicating her opinion that only a nerd would ask about the cost. "I'll bet we could get them for fifty or sixty dollars apiece. That is, if we're ordering in bulk."

Carla's olive complexion suddenly turned an

ashen gray. Fifty or sixty dollars might not mean much to Diana, but getting that kind of money from her parents would be a big deal. "I think that might be a little beyond some of the members' means," she said aloud.

Diana looked annoyed. "You can't do anything worthwhile without money," she snapped. "If you can't get the cash any other way, why don't you get a part-time job and work for it?"

"I have a job already," Carla said evenly. "But I'm saving my earnings for college. Are you saying that because I have to save for my education, I won't be able to go to games with the Pompon Squad anymore?"

"Oh, don't make such a big deal out of it," Diana snapped. "You're just making trouble because you know you wouldn't look good in an aviator jacket anyway. Don't get mad at us just because we think the squad should make a nice appearance."

Carla said nothing. It was true that her figure was chunky. She had already failed to make cheerleading because she was overweight. That she could accept. But why should a few extra pounds keep her from being part of the Pompon Squad? She felt insulted and angry, but she didn't have the nerve to talk back to Diana in front of the others. Maybe Diana was just saying what everyone else secretly felt. If that was true, she wasn't sure she wanted to push the issue.

Bobbie Anderson finally broke the embarrassed silence. "Maybe we could raise the money to buy jackets for the whole squad," she suggested.

"No way," the squad treasurer, Kit Burroughs, put in. "We're already selling popcorn and programs at the home games, and that money is supposed to be for the school athletic fund. Plus we have special projects for charity. It won't look right if we start spending the money on ourselves."

"That doesn't seem right," said Bobbie. "You mean we can raise funds for everyone else, but we can never raise any money for us?"

"I guess so," said Kit.

Bobbie wasn't satisfied. "The football team doesn't have to pay for its uniforms. The basketball team doesn't pay. They all get uniforms free. So how come we can't even have jackets, even if we're willing to raise the money ourselves? Talk about a rotten deal!"

Holly was beginning to feel sorry that she had brought the subject up. She hadn't thought of any of these complications when she was listening to Diana. "Maybe we should table this discussion for another time," she said.

This was one suggestion the entire steering committee could agree on, but the meeting broke up on a sour note. Carla was thinking that if the uniform proposal went through it might just be easier to drop out of the squad altogether. Bobbie was steaming over the idea that the Pompon Squad was a second-class organization. And Kit was unhappy because she was already doing a lot of work as treasurer. She wasn't looking forward to handling the budget for another big project.

Only Diana left the meeting feeling quite

pleased with herself. So far, her plans were working perfectly. There was more to the story about squad uniforms at her old school than she'd bothered to confide to Holly about. By the time the squad had gotten the uniforms, there had been so much squabbling that the squad president was practically forced to resign. The way things were going, Holly might end up in the same kind of trouble. That meant that if somehow one of the girl cheerleaders did have to leave the Varsity Squad, Holly would no longer be the obvious replacement.

And if Plan A didn't work, Diana Tucker could always take over the Tarenton High Pompon Squad.

Savoring this possibility, Diana left the cafeteria early and strolled down the hall in the direction of her next class. On the way, she heard the strains of a single violin coming from the music room. She peeked inside and saw Hope Chang, engrossed in her music.

It was just like Hope to be skipping lunch to practice! Diana thought. Hope was the kind of girl Diana automatically disliked — a goody-goody. Diana never stopped to consider that Hope might have her own reasons for working so hard. Since she herself never did anything at school without some hidden motive, she assumed Hope was the same way.

"Don't tell me you skipped lunch!" Diana said, interrupting Hope's playing.

"Oh no." Hope held up an apple that she was munching on in between stints of practice.

"No wonder you're so thin," Diana said in a concerned voice. "You'd better be careful, though. You don't want to end up sick." She sat down, making it clear that she was in no hurry to let Hope get back to her playing. "Isn't it kind of hard on Peter, though? I just saw him in the lunchroom, and he looked so lonely I had a half a mind to go over and try to cheer him up. But I guess he understands how it is."

Hope looked suspicious. "Understands how what is?"

Diana opened her eyes wide in mock innocence. "That you're so busy. I mean, I guess he's used to amusing himself. Most girls wouldn't leave a boy-friend like that by himself so much."

"I just date Peter, I'm not his keeper!" Hope snapped.

Diana's eyes opened wide. "Don't get upset, Hope. I didn't mean anything personal."

I bet you didn't, Hope thought. "Excuse me, Diana, but if I can't practice, I might as well go have some lunch." Hope locked her violin in the instrument closet and swept out of the room, her shoulders rigid in what she hoped was a demon-stration of dignified disdain. She knew that Diana had just been trying to get a rise out of her.

Why do I always let catty remarks get to me? Hope asked herself. On her way to the cafeteria, she thought of a dozen different replies she could have made that would have put Diana in her place. But she had been brought up to be polite and considerate. When she got into a conversation with someone who wasn't playing by the same rules, more often than not she just couldn't hide the fact that her feelings were hurt.

Back in the music room, Diana was feeling a certain satisfaction. If possible, she disliked Hope even more than she did Olivia. Hope was the kind of girl who would have an entire paragraph under her picture in the high school yearbook. Honor society . . . Varsity Cheerleading . . . orchestra . . . student council, and so on. And on top of all that, she'd probably get voted "Most Likely to Succeed."

It didn't occur to Diana that Hope did these things because she enjoyed them. As far as Diana was concerned, the only reason anyone did anything was to get attention. In her opinion, Hope was just a little show-off. And a greedy one, too, because she wanted to have it all: good grades, cheerleading, and a cute guy besides.

Seething with jealousy, Diana noticed that Hope had left the zippered plastic portfolio she used to carry her sheet music lying on the chair next to her music stand. Impulsively, Diana rifled through the portfolio and stuck the sheet music Hope had been using inside her own oversized hobo bag. Hope thought she was little Miss Perfect, didn't she? Let her see what it felt like to have to cope with a problem!

CHAPTER

"**D**id you hear about the jackets the Pompon Squad is getting?" Jessica asked Olivia as they changed for Tuesday's practice. "Holly is designing them herself."

"That's crazy," Olivia said automatically. "Where are they going to get the money to buy jackets?"

"I don't know. I guess they'll use the money they raise selling programs and stuff at the home games."

"It's going to take a lot of programs to pay for jackets for the whole Pompon Squad," Olivia said. "Besides, that money's all earmarked. Some of it's supposed to go for new practice equipment for the football team. And the rest is for charity. If you ask me, Holly Hudson's getting power-mad. She's forgotten that the Pompon Squad is supposed to support the teams. It's not her own personal kingdom!"

Jessica had finished dressing and was doing some warm-up stretches at the barre that lined one end of the locker room. Watching herself in the mirror, she did a few pliés and then an arabesque.

Years ago, she'd taken ballet classes and loved them. She had never been very graceful though, and she'd quit after one recital when her teacher commented that she looked as if she'd wandered into the ensemble from a touch football game somewhere offstage. Now, looking at herself in the mirror, she realized that she'd grown into the image of a prima ballerina. Her legs had grown long and slender, and her waist was tiny. She was no longer the wiry kid she'd been back in ballet class, and the change felt good. She was feeling especially good today, limber and full of energy. Olivia's objections seemed just plain crabby.

"Oh, come on, Livvy," she urged. "Lighten up. Is it so terrible if the Pompon Squad wants to spend a little money on itself for once?"

"They never did before," Olivia pointed out. "Last year's club didn't mind working for others."

"That was last year," Jessica said.

"So why does it have to be any different this year?" Olivia asked, missing the edge of annoyance in Jessica's voice.

"Well why *shouldn't* it be different?" Jessica balanced herself on the tips of her gym shoes for a few seconds, trying to imagine how she'd look in ballet slippers now.

Olivia was caught unaware. "I didn't think *you'd* be against me!" she gasped.

"Who said anything about being against you? It's just that sometimes we get tired of hearing about how perfect everything was last year."

"I never said things were perfect last year!"

"Okay, I'm sorry. I guess I'm just being touchy," Jessica apologized. She was in no mood to argue, though she did often wonder whether Olivia was again comparing this year's cheerleading squad unfavorably to last year's.

Olivia accepted Jessica's offer of peace, and headed out to the gym. After the coach's lecture last time, she was determined not to let anything interfere with her concentration.

Fortunately, the other members of the squad seemed to feel the same way. They had a new pompon routine to get ready, and Olivia was pleased when her choice of music was accepted without debate. She had heard the jazzed up version of "Alexander's Ragtime Band" played on a jazz-nostalgia show on the community college radio station and taped it, thinking that the familiar, catchy tune would make a good routine. Since everyone knew the melody, it ought to be easy to make up new words and have the Pompon Squad sing along.

Anyway, that had been her idea originally. At the moment, though, it didn't look as if the Pompon Squad and the cheerleaders were going to be cooperating too closely for the rest of the season.

The first time the squad tried to do the new

routine through from beginning to end, it looked pretty ragged. "Not too bad, guys," Olivia encouraged them. "But we need more punch in our jumps. And Jessica, when you do the herkie, remember to keep your fists closed, arms at your waist. This isn't *Swan Lake*."

Instead of being annoyed, Jessica giggled at this, as if Olivia had made some sort of private joke.

Olivia shrugged and led the group through a second run-through. This time everyone did much better. The only real problem was Hope, who didn't seem to have profited much from the last talk. The smile on Hope's face never faltered, not even during the routine's highest kicks. But it looked so artificial that it might have been sprayed out of an aerosol can. If anything, Hope seemed stiffer than ever. Olivia decided not to say anything right now. Everyone had a bad day now and then. She'd give Hope a little time to work out her problem, whatever it was.

"I think that's enough for today," she announced as the last chord of the tape faded out. "We look great, if I do say so myself."

"That's right! Three cheers for us!" Sean piped up, never reluctant to give himself a pat on the back. The others laughed happily and started drifting in the direction of the locker rooms.

"That was a good practice, Olivia," the coach said. "I like the new routine, and you did a good job of teaching it to the squad."

Olivia swallowed hard. There was something she'd been wanting to ask coach Engborg ever since last week's practice, and she knew now that she couldn't avoid it. "Mrs. Engborg, you didn't really tell Diana Tucker that I wasn't a natural leader, did you?" she blurted out.

The coach frowned. "To be absolutely honest, I guess I did say something like that. But I didn't mean it as a criticism. Natural leaders aren't necessarily the best leaders. You've had to overcome shyness. You can empathize with other people's problems. And I think you've been a better captain because of it."

"Oh, uh . . . okay. Thanks, Coach." Olivia backed away from the conversation as quickly as possible. She had been so sure that Ardith Engborg would deny ever having said any such thing that she was almost in shock. The way the coach explained it, she hadn't meant to be negative. But Olivia wondered if the explanation was sincere. Maybe the coach regretted being so candid to a newcomer like Diana, and was just trying to make amends.

She wished that Duffy was around this evening, but unfortunately he was covering a junior varsity hockey match halfway across the county and wouldn't be getting back home until late. Instead she accepted Tara's offer of a lift home in the Chevy.

Tara had been unusually friendly lately, and tonight was no exception. Before her car's engine had even had a chance to warm up, Tara started talking.

"I think all cars should have nicknames don't you?" she said, almost talking to herself.

"Sure," agreed Olivia, who wasn't sure she thought so at all.

"I guess I'll call this one Velvet. Can you guess why?"

"Because it runs so smoothly?

"Good guess, but not what I had in mind. It's after *National Velvet*. You know, the story about the steeplechase horse. When I was younger that was my favorite movie. The old version of course, the one with Elizabeth Taylor in it. You wouldn't believe how pretty Elizabeth Taylor was when she was young! I'd kill to have violet eyes like hers! Anyway, in the story, the horse is supposed to be all washed up. . . ."

Olivia sat in silence, listening to Tara ramble on. Tara was a tall girl, and she was wearing jeans and high boots that accentuated her voluptuous figure. On top, she wore a hand-knit sweater and matching cap in a bright gold color. Her red hair hung loose under the cap, framing her face. Olivia felt she ought to keep up her end of the conversation, but as usual she found Tara's presence a little bit overwhelming. Tara had everything in the looks department, and now she wanted Elizabeth Taylor's eyes, too! It was hard to sympathize.

Nevertheless, Olivia suspected that Tara was exactly the kind of person Coach Engborg had in mind when she talked about natural leadership ability. For the hundredth time, she wondered what she, Olivia Evans, was doing in the role of squad captain when Tara could no doubt fill the job with ease.

Was it possible that Coach Engborg, in her tactful way, was suggesting that Olivia ought to step aside and let someone else take over?

That's a ridiculous idea! Olivia told herself. I shouldn't even think such a thing. But now that the idea had occurred to her, it was going to be hard to push it out of her mind.

Normally, Peter Rayman could change out of his practice clothes, shower, and dress in six minutes, tops. Today, however, he was taking his time, making sure that Hope would be long gone from school before he ventured out of the boys' locker room.

He had already told Hope that he had to stay late to finish a chemistry experiment, and it was hard enough telling her one lie. He didn't want to run into her now and have to repeat it.

Technically, he assured himself, what he'd told Hope wasn't a lie at all. It just wasn't the whole truth. He did have a chem experiment to finish. But the experiment didn't happen to be his. It was Diana Tucker's.

Diana was in his chemistry class, and she was having a tough time keeping up with the work. He didn't see that he'd done anything wrong by volunteering to help her after school, but something had warned him that Hope wouldn't like it. For some reason, all the girls seemed to be against Diana, and Hope was no exception. If she was going to be so unreasonable, Peter figured, then he was justified in not telling her everything.

Diana was waiting in the chem lab when he

arrived. "It's wonderful of you to help me out," she told him. "I guess I'm just an awful dummy when it comes to science. And this is nothing like the stuff we were doing at my last school."

Peter glanced at the equipment he'd helped her set up during class, and realized that Diana hadn't even started the experiment. "What happened?" he asked, startled. "I showed you the first steps. Did you have trouble right at the beginning?"

"I don't know." Diana shrugged helplessly. "I guess I just got confused. I was thinking that maybe you'd let me copy your results. Just this once."

For a brief instant, it occurred to Peter that he was being used. Diana hadn't tried to do the work at all. And she didn't want to try.

But Diana looked so beautiful that it was hard to concentrate on staying angry. She was wearing a V-neck sweater in a turquoise color that made her eyes look even bigger and bluer than usual. And the faint aroma of her cologne was making it hard for him to think straight.

"It's been hard to concentrate on schoolwork," Diana said. "No one around here seems to like me. I've been so miserable."

"People will like you. You just have to give them a chance."

"Do you really think so?" Diana's lower lip quivered. "So far, you're the only person I've met here who I can talk to. But, then, you're not like the others. You're so much more mature."

"I'm glad you think so," mumbled Peter. Mentally, he was kicking himself for not being able to come up with a better reply. He wasn't used to thinking of himself as the mature type, especially where girls were concerned. Living alone with a divorced mother could be tough. He often wished that he had an older brother. Or that his dad didn't live hundreds of miles away with his new wife and kids.

"I really need a strong shoulder to cry on," Diana said, her blue eyes brimming with tears. "Do you think we could go somewhere quiet? Just to talk, I mean."

She put her hand on Peter's shoulder, then hurriedly pulled it away. "I guess I forgot about Hope. I'm sure she wouldn't approve of us being together. I wouldn't want to get you in any trouble."

The way Diana said it made Peter feel embarrassed and resentful. Hope didn't own him. They weren't even officially going steady.

"You won't get me in trouble," he said defiantly. "It's still a free country, last I heard."

On their way out of the school building they stopped at Diana's locker. As he was helping Diana into her rabbit fur coat, Peter happened to notice some crumpled sheet music lying on the floor of her locker. He had seen enough of Hope's music to recognize a violin arrangement, and he was surprised.

"I didn't realize you played the violin!" he exclaimed.

"Huh?" Diana followed his glance and then hastily slammed the door of her locker. "Oh, yes, I do. I was going to try out for the orchestra, but

Mr. Martin said I'd just be wasting my time. He seemed awfully hostile. It was almost as if someone had been telling him bad things about me."

Diana didn't say so, but she was obviously hinting that the "someone" in question had been Hope Chang. Peter couldn't believe that Hope would bad-mouth another student to a teacher. That wouldn't be like her at all. On the other hand, he had noticed that Hope got a funny look in her eyes whenever Diana's name was mentioned.

"Let's not talk about boring old school stuff now," Diana said as they left the school and walked across the parking lot to her car. "Let's talk about you and me."

CHAPTER

At about seven o'clock that same evening, Jessica was in her room trying to study when she looked out the window and saw Pres Tilford's red Porsche pulling into her driveway. Irrationally, her first thought was that Pres was coming to tell her that something had happened to Patrick. Had he been hurt? Was he in the hospital again?

Her heart pounding, she raced through the kitchen and out the back door. She was practically standing beside the Porsche before she realized that the driver was Patrick himself, almost unrecognizable in flannel slacks, a tweed jacket and tie, and, of all things, a Stetson hat, which he wore pulled down over one eye at a rakish angle.

"Patrick! What happened! What's going on?" she blurted out.

He flashed a wicked grin, the same old Patrick in spite of the dressy clothes. "I realize I've cleaned up my act a bit, but there's no need to be alarmed. The change isn't that drastic."

"Oh, yes it is," Jessica contradicted him. "And what are you doing in Pres's car? I can't believe he'd lend it, even to you."

"That's where you're wrong. I know it's out of character, but Pres decided to trust me with it for once. In view of this being a special occasion."

"It is?"

"It is, provided that you haven't had dinner yet."

"As a matter of fact, we haven't. This is the evening Mom works late at Marnie's. She just got home a few minutes ago. And my stepdad is out of town on business." Jessica was starting to think she'd lost her mind. "Patrick, were we supposed to go somewhere together? Did I forget?"

"We're going to dinner at Chez Marcel. That is, if you'll do me the honor of coming with me, Miss Jessica." A bit belatedly, he picked up the single red rosebud wrapped in tissue paper that was lying on the passenger seat beside him and thrust it into Jessica's hands. "But you didn't forget," he added. "I just thought I'd surprise you."

Jessica stared at the rose, then back at Patrick. "But why? What's this all about?"

Patrick laughed. "You are one difficult girl to impress, Jessica Bennett. Here I am trying to make a romantic gesture, and you're looking at me very suspiciously."

"Oh, I'm impressed." Jessica protested. "I love it. I love — " She almost said, "I love you," but caught herself just in time. "I mean, I'd love to go. It's just that I can't help wondering why you picked tonight."

"No special reason. Except that I've been working so much lately, we hardly see each other. And because it occurred to me that I never take you out anywhere nice."

Patrick didn't mention it, but he was also thinking about Jessica's flirtation with Charles Alexander during the squad's trip to New Orleans. Suave, wealthy Charles had courted Jessica with gifts of imported chocolates and taken her out for lunch to the best French restaurant in town.

Luckily for Patrick, Charles's personality didn't live up to the same standard as his A-one financial rating. But the episode had made Patrick resolve not to take Jessica for granted from now on. Jessica's beautiful green eyes, not to mention her unspoiled good nature, were going to attract the attention of other Charleses in the future. And Patrick was determined to prove that if Jessica stuck with him there would be more to life than chowing down on take-out hamburgers in the cab of his moving van.

Once she'd had a chance to get over her shock, Jessica was delighted with Patrick's surprise invitation. All that remained was for her to explain the situation to her mother and change into something dressy. Jessica thought immediately of the green silk dress she'd bought to wear when her brother John appeared in a play at the junior college. Patrick had never seen her in it, and she'd been waiting for a chance to show it off to him.

Getting Mrs. Bennett's approval was more of an obstacle. "Patrick must be even more irresponsible than I thought," Mrs. Bennett said when she heard where Jessica was going. "In fact, you probably won't even be able to get a table. Many evenings you can't even get into Chez Marcel without a reservation."

"Patrick thought of that," Jessica explained. "He's already called ahead for a reservation. And I don't see what's so irresponsible about going out to dinner. It's a little bit impulsive, maybe."

"I suppose it's all right for you to go," Abby Bennett allowed. "But this kind of thing just makes me feel more strongly than ever that Patrick is too old for you."

"He's only a year older!" Jessica pointed out. "That's hardly a big age difference, Mom. What am I supposed to do, only go out without guys who were born in the same month as I was?"

Abby Bennett frowned. "Of course not. Don't be silly. But age is relative. I wouldn't mind if Patrick were a freshman at the junior college. But he's not a student. You know very well, it's just that I don't want to see you getting too involved while you're still in school."

"I'm not involved," Jessica insisted, wondering to herself if that was really the truth. "It's just a date."

"Yes, I suppose it is."

Mrs. Bennett looked as if she had more to say

on the subject, but Jessica was bursting with impatience. "Is it okay if I go get dressed now?" she said, practically bolting for her room. "Our reservation is for eight o'clock."

Her mom smiled. "I guess so. And dear . . . if you want to wear my gold earrings, go ahead."

Jessica gave a little shriek of joy and rushed off to her room while Mrs. Bennett went out to the living room to entertain Patrick.

Fortunately, Jessica wasn't like Tara, who would have needed at least three hours to get ready for a dress up date . . . or like Olivia, who would have changed her mind at least three times before deciding on an outfit . . . or even like Hope, who didn't particularly enjoy surprises. In a matter of minutes, she had showered and brushed her hair and was slipping into the green silk dress. Her mother's good earrings and a touch of pink lipstick were all it took to complete her transformation.

Patrick greeted her entrance into the living room with an exaggerated wolf whistle. "I shoulda known you were one of those classy dames all along," he added, slipping into his Bogart imitation, which was surprisingly good.

Mrs. Bennett raised her eyes to the ceiling, doing her best to hide her appreciation of Patrick's charm. But she couldn't help smiling.

"Why does your mother think I'm irresponsible?" Patrick asked, as soon as they had pulled out of the Bennett driveway. "Not that I meant to eavesdrop, but I couldn't help it."

"I'm sure she doesn't really think that," Jessica

said. "You know mothers, they have to have something to complain about."

Actually, Jessica thought that it was the *responsible* side of Patrick's personality that bothered her mother. He'd been out of high school for only a few months, so he hardly qualified as an older man. But H&T's TLC Moving, the company he'd formed with Pres Tilford, was already a success. Patrick was independent. He knew what he wanted out of life, and was used to going all out to get it. Jessica could hardly blame her mother for worrying that she and Patrick might get serious too quickly. It worried her, too, sometimes.

When she didn't see Patrick for a few days, Jessica would make all sorts of resolutions about keeping their relationship from getting too intense. Then he'd show up unexpectedly, the way he had tonight, and the resolutions would recede to the back of her mind. Patrick was sexy all right. But it was more than that — when she was with him, she felt a warmth and tenderness that she'd never felt before. Of course, he also had a few rough edges that even new clothes and a borrowed Porsche couldn't disguise.

For one thing, when the time came for them to order dinner at Chez Marcel, it was obvious that Patrick didn't have a clue as to what any of items on the French menu might be. And he was too proud to let Jessica help him out. Almost defiantly, he ordered a steak and French fries, the same dinner he could have had at half a dozen less expensive places in the area.

Jessica, who'd learned a bit about French restaurants during her visit to New Orleans, decided to be adventurous. "I'll have the *grenouilles*," she told the waiter.

"Very good, miss," he said with approval.

When the food arrived some minutes later, Patrick peered at her plate with interest. "Good grief," he barked, in a voice loud enough to be heard several tables away, "those gree-nyou-whee whatcha-ma-callits look just like frogs!"

It seemed to Jessica that every pair of eyes in the room was focused right on their table. One older woman with white hair picked up her napkin and held it in front of her mouth to disguise a minor fit of giggles.

"That's exactly what they are," Jessica hissed. "Frogs' legs."

"Well, excuse me," Patrick said.

No doubt this Charles Alexander person knew all about frogs' legs, he thought. It was beginning to dawn on him that in bringing Jessica to Chez Marcel he was trying to compete with a rival who was already out of Jessica's life. And he wasn't doing too well at it, either.

"If you like that stuff, fine. But you've got to realize that my idea of exotic food is a Mexican-style TV dinner," he said.

"Okay. I don't mind your making fun of my order," Jessica answered in a low voice. "But do you have to talk so loud that the whole room hears you? This isn't a performance. It's embarrassing."

"Oh, come on, Jessica. No one heard."

Since the white-haired woman was still looking their way, this obviously wasn't true. Patrick
returned the woman's stare by smiling broadly
and waving in her direction. Even Jessica couldn't
help giggling at how smoothly the woman averted
her eyes, pretending not to notice Patrick's wave.

"See?" said Patrick. "Even if they do notice, it
doesn't make any difference. It's not as if we're
going to see anyone here that we know."

"I wouldn't bet on that," Jessica told him. She
had just spotted two familiar faces across the
room, a sight that made her forget all about her
irritation with Patrick.

Patrick followed Jessica's glance with his
own. "Well, look at that!" he exclaimed under his
breath. "I thought Peter Rayman was going out
with Hope. What do you suppose he's doing in a
place like this with Diana Tucker?"

Peter, seated across from Diana in a secluded
booth along the wall, was wondering the same
thing. When Diana suggested going somewhere
quiet to talk, this wasn't exactly what he'd had in
mind.

After leaving school, they had driven around
aimlessly in Diana's car for a while, until she
happened to mention this "cute little place" she'd
noticed a few days earlier. *Cute* was not a word
that Peter associated with Chez Marcel. *Expensive* was more like it. But when he'd finally realized that it was what Diana had in mind, he'd
been too embarrassed to say anything. Diana
Tucker obviously wasn't the kind of girl who was

69

used to being taken out for a hamburger or a slice of pizza.

Peter had ordered a salad, the cheapest item on the menu, while Diana got an expensive veal dish that she hardly touched. But for that matter, he couldn't eat, either. His emotions were on a see-saw. One minute, he was worrying about the bill and resenting Diana for putting him in such an awkward situation. The next, he was over-whelmed with the thought that this beautiful girl seemed to be crazy about him.

"I just don't know how I would have survived in Tarenton if I hadn't met you," Diana told him, giving his hand a squeeze. "I've been trying to make friends here, but so far everyone seems to be against me. I guess I'm just too sophisticated for Tarenton."

At that moment, Peter looked up and saw Patrick and Jessica watching him from their table across the room. A wave of guilt swept over him. He'd been trying not to think about Hope, and where she fit in — or, rather, didn't fit in — to this new development in his life. But the expression of surprise and disapproval on Jessica's face reminded him that nothing was a secret in Tarenton for long.

Then he thought about Sean. Sean Dubrow was always moving from one girl to another. And did he feel guilty? Not that Peter could tell. What's more, everyone seemed to accept Sean's role as Mr. Macho of Tarenton High. What would Sean do in a situation like this? Certainly not try to hide.

"Excuse me," he said to Diana. "I've got to say hello to my friends. I'll be right back."

After greeting Jessica, Peter asked Patrick if they could talk privately out in the entrance hall. Patrick was feeling prosperous, and responded to Peter's request for a loan by handing over two crisp twenty-dollar bills. "I'd appreciate it if you don't mention to Hope that you saw me here," Peter said with a wink. He hoped his man-of-the-world act was more convincing than it felt, but Patrick, at least, seemed to be buying it.

"You can count on us not to say anything," Patrick told him. "But that doesn't mean Hope won't find out you were here."

"Of course she will," Peter assured him. "I plan to tell her myself." He couldn't remember telling so many lies in one day since the time he broke the garage window playing baseball when he was ten years old. What was scary was that this time he was starting to see how easy it was to lie.

Jessica didn't have much time to wonder what Peter and Patrick were talking about out in the entrance hall. Almost as soon as they departed, another familiar face came into view — Else Gunderson, the owner of Marnie's boutique and her mother's boss.

"Jessica Bennett, what a surprise!" Else exclaimed, descending on Jessica with a big hug. "You look charming . . . so grown-up!"

Jessica wasn't sure that being told she looked "grown-up" was such a terrific compliment. When a person really looked grown-up, adults didn't go out of their way to comment on it. But Else meant well. She introduced Jessica to the out-of-town buyer she was about to have dinner with, and the three of them chatted pleasantly for a few minutes.

"Jessica was one of the models in the fashion show I was telling you about," Else told the buyer. "Even though we're far from New York and L.A., we're up with the latest trends. The young girls today have such marvelous fashion sense.

"I was just telling Mr. Crossley about Mary Ellen Kirkwood," Else added for Jessica's benefit. "I suppose you've heard. Mary Ellen's thinking about moving back here to Tarenton. If she does, I may take her on as a buyer. I could use some advice on what the high school set is wearing, and Mary Ellen has such a wonderful eye for clothes."

"She sure does," Jessica agreed, a lump rising in her throat.

By the time Patrick returned to the table, Else Gunderson and Mr. Crossley had moved on.

"I just saw Mrs. Gunderson, and you'll never guess what she told me," Jessica said, trying to sound casual. "Mary Ellen Kirkwood might be coming back to town."

"That's right," agreed Patrick.

"You knew about it?"

"Uh . . . I'd heard something like that."

"But how? Who told you?"

Patrick wished he'd had enough sense to keep his big mouth shut. "Actually, I got a letter from Mary Ellen, and she mentioned something about that. I was going to tell you, but it slipped my mind."

"Slipped your mind! Do you expect me to believe that?"

"Don't look at me that way," Patrick said. "I didn't ask Mary Ellen to write me. What am I supposed to do, put a lock on my mailbox? Besides, Mary Ellen is an old friend. And *I'm* not the one who was down in New Orleans having a great time with someone else."

"But that was different!" Jessica protested. "I was never serious about Charles."

"I don't see why it's so different," Patrick shot back.

But looking at the hurt in her green eyes, he couldn't stay angry for long. "Come on, Jessica," he cajoled, "let's not spoil the evening by arguing. Mary Ellen and I are history. Let's start living in the present."

Jessica knew that Patrick believed what he was saying. Still, she couldn't help wondering whether Mary Ellen had been informed that she and Patrick were finished. If she had, then why was she still writing him letters?

She had never wanted to fall in love in the first place. After her own father died suddenly of a heart attack, she realized how lonely and lost she'd felt. And she had concluded that the best way to avoid that kind of grief and suffering was to avoid caring too much about any one person. It was Patrick who had made her forget the dangers of getting involved. He was always so sure of himself, so confident that everything would work out beautifully if only they just trusted each other. . . .

It hurt to be reminded that Patrick had once felt just as sure of his feelings for Mary Ellen Kirkwood. That romance hadn't worked out, at least not at the time, so what made her think that she would be any luckier?

Jessica did her best to put all those confusing thoughts out of her mind and enjoy the rest of the evening, but they simply refused to go away.

CHAPTER

Olivia was crossing the Tarenton High cafeteria, balancing a tray loaded with several pieces of fruit, a glass of milk, and a portion of Wednesday's menu special, a concoction that the students had nicknamed "gruesome stew," when she narrowly missed colliding with Andy Poletti.

"Hey, Livvy!" said Andy, who was cheerfully balancing his own tray on the tips of the fingers of his right hand. "Did you hear about the custom-tailored jackets the Pompon Squad is getting?"

"If one more person asks me that, I think I'll scream," Olivia snapped.

Andy's smile crumpled. "I didn't realize it was a sore subject. Forget I mentioned it."

"Sorry, Andy," Olivia apologized. "It's just that the Pompon Squad and the cheerleaders aren't cooperating too well these days. It's too bad your sister isn't still here. She was always more tactful than I."

"Angie could be a diplomat if she wanted," Andy agreed with pride. "But I'm sure you can work everything out on your own. After all, you're the feisty type."

Small, slender Olivia wasn't used to thinking of herself as feisty, and Andy's remark made her feel good. Still, she wasn't sure how feistiness was going to resolve the disagreement between Holly Hudson and the cheerleaders. Holly was still angry about the reception her card stunts had received, and now she wanted to be master of ceremonies at Friday's pep rally, replacing Olivia.

According to Holly, a pep rally was really a Pompon Squad activity, and so the president of the squad ought to be in charge. It did no good to remind her that the cheerleaders had been selected for their ability to motivate crowds. It did no good to remind her that the cheerleaders' captain had always led rallies in the past. When Holly wanted something, she would never let mere logic stand in her way.

And so far, Coach Engborg had been no help at all. When Olivia appealed to her, the coach just smiled and said that she was sure Olivia would be able to handle the situation without her intervention. Olivia couldn't help suspecting that her leadership was being put to some sort of test. Perhaps the coach was already planning to dump her for another captain, and just wanted to demonstrate that Olivia was a complete flop.

Her mind reeling with the implications of the

coach's attitude, Olivia made her way to a quiet table at the rear of the cafeteria. Jessica, Tara, and Hope were already settled there, having volunteered to help her write some new words to the song they were using for the pompon routine.

Tara was the only member of the group who showed any enthusiasm for the job. "I've been thinking about this ever since our last practice," she announced as soon as Olivia sat down. "How about: 'Come on along, come on along, we're the best school in the land. . . .' "

Tara stood up to sing the words, her shoulders thrown back and her red hair flying as she strutted in place. She had a clear, penetrating voice, and even though she wasn't trying to project, it could be heard throughout the back section of the cafeteria. Everyone turned to look, and there was scattered applause from a few tables nearby. Tara raised her arms in acknowledgment, and then sat down, feeling quite pleased with herself. "See?" she said. "It's a success already."

"But what are the rest of the lyrics?" asked Hope innocently.

"Oh, that's as far as I got."

Olivia rolled her eyes in amazement. "You thought about this for two days, and that's as far as you got! All you did was substitute the word *school* for *band* in the original lyrics."

Tara shrugged. "Okay, so I didn't exactly have a brainstorm. But at least I'm trying. I haven't heard any fantastic ideas from the rest of you. In fact, you all look as if we're planning a funeral, not a pep rally."

"You're right," Jessica admitted. "I'm afraid I'm not in a very good mood today."

"Is something wrong?" asked Tara.

There was, but Jessica didn't feel like discussing it. "Not really," she said. "Patrick took me to Chez Marcel last night for dinner."

Tara giggled. "*That's* your problem? Half the girls in school would kill to get an evening at Chez Marcel with Patrick Henley."

"I guess I'm just tired," Jessica lied. "I'm not used to having big dates on school nights, and I didn't sleep very well."

"My problem is a lot more serious than that," Hope blurted out.

Jessica wanted to kick herself. When she mentioned Chez Marcel she'd forgotten all about seeing Peter there with Diana. No wonder Hope was upset! "Don't let it get you down," she said, giving Hope a sympathetic pat on the shoulder. "The male sex can't be trusted. The only way to survive is not to let yourself care too much about any one of them. There are always other fish in the sea."

Hope's dark eyes widened in confusion. "I don't know what you're talking about," she said. "My problem's got nothing to with the male sex. Or with fish, for that matter. It's just that I've mislaid the sheet music for my solo. I can't practice until I find it, and I don't want to have to tell Mr. Martin that it's lost. I worked so hard to show him that I could handle music and cheerleading, too, and now this could undo everything."

"Just because you lost a few pieces of paper?" asked Tara.

Hope looked miserable. "The thing is, I have no idea what happened to it. I was sure I left it in the orchestra room in my portfolio, but when I got home last night it was gone. And this morning, I did a dumb thing. I thought I'd find the music somewhere, maybe in one of my classrooms, so I told Mr. Martin that the reason I was skipping my usual practice before homeroom was that I have a cold. Now if I don't find the music, he'll put two and two together and realize that I lied."

None of them could think of a reason why anyone would want to steal sheet music, especially since Hope was the only violinist in school good enough to play that particular piece.

"And I won't be good enough to play it, either, if I don't find it soon and start practicing," Hope wailed.

This time, Jessica managed to keep her mouth shut. It was obvious that Hope didn't know anything about Peter's date with Diana, and she had enough problems at the moment without hearing the news. Of course, she was sure to find out sooner or later. Peter hadn't looked as if he would be able to keep his interest in Diana a secret indefinitely.

She was still trying to decide whether she ought to tell Hope after all, when Olivia changed the subject. "We've got to try to put our personal problems aside and figure out what we're going to do about Friday's pep rally," she reminded the others. "At the moment, I'm more worried about Holly than about writing the words to a new spirit song. If she doesn't get her way, she could turn the entire Pompon Squad against us."

"Maybe you're being too hard on her," suggested Tara. "Holly means well, and it almost seems as if you're against every idea she has. Everyone knows you're dead set against the squad getting jackets. I can't see what's so wrong with it, myself. Think of what a great impression all those matching jackets in one section would make on kids from other schools."

"It just won't work," Olivia countered. "There's no way that the squad can raise that much money. The only way it can be done is if the members pay for their own jackets, and a lot of them can't afford that."

"So what's the big deal?" Tara wondered. "Why can't the members with money buy their own jackets, and the squad treasury subsidize the rest?"

Olivia shook her head. "I say it won't work. No one wants to be a charity case. I know a couple of kids are already thinking of quitting if that happens. Besides, I have a funny feeling that someone is whispering ideas in Holly's ear. She's the kind of person who's easily influenced."

"And I know just who that someone is," Tara announced triumphantly. "It's Diana Tucker."

"Maybe you're right," Olivia said, "but we shouldn't be too quick to jump to conclusions. This is only Diana's second week in school. No one moves that fast."

"I don't know about that," put in Jessica. Privately, she knew that Diana was causing trouble in more areas than one. Still, she wasn't sure that she could trust her judgment on the subject. Maybe the real reason she didn't like Diana was because of her resemblance to Mary Ellen Kirkwood. And after all, she didn't know the full story of Diana's date with Peter.

"I agree with Jessica and Olivia," Hope Chang said. "I don't much like Diana, either, but that doesn't mean she's to blame for the Pompon Squad situation. There's no reason to think she would stir up trouble deliberately. Let's give her a chance."

"That's fine with me," said Tara. "I can take care of myself. But just don't say that I didn't warn the rest of you."

With a toss of her head, Tara departed.

"Who does she think she is?" Jessica asked. "Wonder Woman?"

Olivia smiled to herself. That was exactly who Tara sometimes reminded her of. She was pretty sure that underneath all that bravado, Tara wasn't as tough as she liked to think she was. On the other hand, she often wished that she was as good an actress as Tara could be. A little bit of that ability would come in handy in dealing with Holly Hudson.

At the Pompon Squad meeting that was being held in the gym that same lunch hour, Holly was having problems of her own.

Normally, only fifteen or twenty members showed up for the regular scheduled meetings of the squad. More students rode the Pompon Squad buses to the away games and sat in the Pompon Squad cheering section at home, but there was really only a small core of members who could be counted on to do the hard work — decorating the gym for rallies, organizing the program and popcorn sales, and running the squad's program of visiting hospital patients and shut-ins.

At first, Holly was delighted to see that attendance at today's meeting had nearly tripled. Diana's idea about getting jackets for the squad was really paying off, she thought. The section of the bleachers where the squad usually met was filled to overflowing. And a lot of the new faces were freshmen and sophomores, people who had never so much as attended a game before.

"It's great to see such a large turnout," Holly said, calling the meeting to order. "I think we should start by hearing Carla's report on the shut-in visitation program. Then we can get on to the fun part of the session, the planning for Friday's rally."

Carla stood up and started to give her report, doing her best to ignore the chatter and disruptions in the seats a few rows back. But the more she tried to continue, the more unruly her audience became.

Finally, Holly couldn't take it any more. "What's going on back there?" she bellowed. "Pipe down and let Carla talk."

"But this stuff is boring," one of the freshman girls answered back.

"That's right," said another. "We didn't come

to hear about hospital visits. When are we going to discuss getting our jackets?"

Holly was exasperated. "We agreed to table that subject for a week."

"Then let's *un*table it," the girl said. "I make a motion that we take whatever money is in the treasury and put it toward buying jackets for everyone who's here today."

"I second that," yelled a sophomore.

"Wait just a second. Hold on!" Holly shouted back. "You can't do that. You aren't even a Pompon Squad member. I've never seen you before. I don't even know your name."

"So what?" said the sophomore. "Is there some kind of rule that says no one can be an official member of the squad without your permission?"

Holly looked beseechingly at Carla, who was the squad secretary. Surely there was some rule in the squad's bylaws that would cover this situation. There must be some way to limit who was entitled to vote at meetings.

But Carla just shook her head. "We never anticipated anything like this," she told Holly. "Our problem has always been getting kids to come out to meetings, not stopping them from coming."

"See," said the first freshman. "Let's vote on the motion right now. All in favor of putting the Pompon Squad treasury toward buying jackets for everyone present right now, say 'aye.'"

There was a loud chorus of ayes, mostly from the newcomers in the back rows. The stalwarts of the squad stared at each other in disgust.

"I never dreamed that it would turn out this way," Holly wailed as the meeting broke up in confusion.

"I don't see why not," said Carla quietly. "You thought it was a good idea for us regular members to give ourselves jackets. Why shouldn't the others want to get in on the action?"

Diana, who had been standing silently on the sidelines, suddenly wheeled around and looked at Carla accusingly. "That's the kind of attitude that's responsible for causing all this trouble in the first place. If it weren't for your nit-picking complaints, the squad would have voted on those jackets at the executive meeting, before any of these kids heard anything about it. It's people like you who ruin a good thing for everyone else."

Carla was a quiet girl who worked hard and could usually manage to get along with everybody. Holly relied on Carla to handle a lot of the boring details of running the squad, and she had never heard Carla complain. But this time, Carla was fed up.

"I'm not taking the blame for this fiasco," she said, dumping her minutes book into Holly's limp hands. "If that's the way you feel, you can go all by yourself and try to explain this to Mrs. Engborg."

"Hey, wait a second . . ." Holly wailed as Carla made her exit. "I didn't say anything."

"Oh, let her go," Diana said, tugging at Holly's sleeve. "Who needs her? Girls who look like that shouldn't be allowed in the Pompon Squad, anyway. It's bad for the image of the school. Come on, let's go out to the mall and do some shopping. I saw some great belts out there the other day, in a style that would look great on you."

Holly wasn't sure she agreed with Diana's opinions on what was good for Tarenton High's image. But she felt nervous about disagreeing. If she stuck up for Carla, wouldn't that make Diana think less of her, too? "Okay, let's go," she said without much enthusiasm. "I guess you're right. And if Mrs. Engborg doesn't like the squad's decision, that's her problem."

CHAPTER

Sean Dubrow added another twenty pounds in weights to the Nautilus machine and settled down to do another fifteen thigh presses. He felt good, as he always did when he found the time to work out in the Nautilus room of Pineland Spa. He knew he looked good, too. But, unfortunately, his looks were wasted for the moment on the spa clientele, mostly older men and women.

Sean's father had purchased a "family" membership in the spa, on the theory that he and Sean would be able to use the facilities together. But so far, it hadn't worked out that way. Mark Dubrow was a salesman for Tarenton Fabricators and a widower who enjoyed a busy social life. Now that Sean was a senior and had a busy schedule of his own, the two of them hardly saw each other for days on end.

No one at Tarenton High would have ever

thought of Sean Dubrow as lonely, but sometimes he did get awfully tired of hanging around the big, rambling Dubrow house all by himself. Mrs. Windsor, the motherly housekeeper that he and his father had nicknamed Windy, was usually gone for the day by the time he got home from cheerleading practice and after-school activities. So unless he had a date, there were long evenings to fill with no company except the TV set and the stereo.

One thing Sean liked about the spa was that it was open late. Even though there was seldom anyone around close to his own age, other than the staff, it was a place where he could go to be surrounded by bright lights and real live human voices when the empty house started to drive him crazy.

Tonight, however, he was not going to have to do without someone to talk to. As he was finishing up his work on the leg press machine, he saw a familiar form reflected in the mirrors that lined the workout room. Diana Tucker, the new girl in school, was wearing a lavender leotard, cut high in the hips to accentuate her long, lean legs. When she paused in the doorway to survey the room, all eyes gravitated in her direction.

Sean was at her side in a minute. "Hi, there," he said. "I've seen you around school. You're Diana Tucker, aren't you?"

"That's right," said Diana, not bothering to acknowledge that she was aware of Sean's name.

"Is this your first time here? Can I show you how to use the machines?"

Diana flashed a pouty smile. "I know how to use them. We had Nautilus machines in the school gym in California. But if you want to help me, I don't mind."

Diana followed Sean on a circuit around the room, waiting silently as he adjusted the weights and the height of the seats for her. She did the exercises quickly, putting in so few repetitions on each machine that Sean was almost working harder than she was.

But Sean didn't mind. Ever since the day Diana appeared at Tarenton, he'd assumed that sooner or later he and Diana would be going out on a date together. Attracting girls had never been Sean's problem. Sooner or later, almost everyone went out with him.

So when the workout was finished, Sean naturally invited Diana down to the juice bar. He found a table for them and asked the waitress to bring two Pineland pineapple cocktails, a non-alcoholic drink that was mostly pineapple juice and soda water.

Diana tasted her drink without enthusiasm. "This is canned juice," she said, pushing the glass aside. "In California we always had fresh juice."

"I guess you must really miss the warm weather. You know, they say Tarenton only has two seasons, winter and the Fourth of July."

"Really?" asked Diana, her face dead-pan.

"That was supposed to be a joke," Sean pointed out.

"Oh, see, I didn't know because — "

"I know," Sean interrupted. "In California, you had funnier jokes."

Diana thought this over. She had no sense of humor, but she wasn't easy to insult, either. "I guess we did," she agreed finally.

"The North Country can be beautiful, too," Sean struggled on. "We have some great scenery. And terrific skiing."

"Oh, I'm an expert skier," Diana volunteered. "I'll have to get Peter to take me."

"Peter!" Sean was completely floored. "How about me?"

Diana opened her blue eyes wide. "Didn't you know? Peter and I are going to be going steady."

Of course, Jessica had been absolutely right in predicting that news of Peter and Diana's date at Chez Marcel would get around school before long. In fact, the story had traveled so far in twenty-four hours that Diana herself had to be responsible. But Sean was one of those who hadn't heard a word about it. He had never been much interested in gossip about other people's love lives.

Still, he had seen Peter in class that very day. And at cheerleading practice the day before. "That's funny," he said aloud. "Peter didn't mention that the two of you were an item."

Diana shrugged. "I don't know why not."

"Of course," she added as an afterthought, "he may not realize it yet."

Sean didn't know what to think about that. It didn't especially bother him that he was being rejected, though. No one asked out as many girls as he did without getting turned down from time to time. What made Sean different from most other boys his age was that it never occurred to him that rejection had anything to do with him personally. If a girl didn't find him irresistible, it was probably a sign that she had bad taste.

Driving home from the spa, Sean found himself thinking about Hope. She must be awfully broken up about Peter leaving her for Diana. It was only nine-thirty, not too late to stop by her house and offer her a shoulder to cry on.

Sean made a U-turn at the next intersection, and headed back in the direction of Hope's house.

Hope was sitting by the butcher block table in the Changs' ultramodern eat-in kitchen, thumbing through the Yellow Pages in search of music stores. So far, what she'd found was not very promising. There were a few listings for stores that sold sheet music, but most of them carried just a few pop titles and old standards. None had a big enough stock to do her any good.

One woman had actually laughed out loud when Hope called to ask if they carried violin music. "Honey," she snorted, "we don't know anything about that stuff here. If Madonna can't sing to it, we don't sell it. You'll have to try Scovill's."

"Thanks, anyway," said Hope, hanging up the phone. Scovill's was a large music store located in the big regional mall in Warrenton, over sixty miles away. Even if they did have the piece she needed in stock, how would she ever get there?

Hope went into the study, a spacious, plant-filled room where her mother worked at painting watercolors. "Mom, do you think you could drive me over to Warrenton on Saturday?"

"I'm afraid not, dear," Mrs. Chang said. "I've made an appointment to have the transmission looked at on Saturday morning, and that's one chore that really can't wait. Otherwise, we won't be using the car next week at all."

"Mom, this is really important. . . ."

"So are these repairs, or I wouldn't refuse you." Mrs. Chang looked concerned. "Is something wrong? Why do you need to go to Warrenton?"

"Forget it. If we can't get there, then we can't."

There was no point in explaining her problem to her mother. She would only advise going to Mr. Martin for help. And anyway, Hope wasn't even sure that Mr. Martin had an extra copy of the music for her solo. The sheet music she'd been using had come from his private music library to begin with, and he'd made a point of getting her to promise that she would take good care of it.

Hope went into her bedroom and began rummaging through her book shelves and dresser drawers. She looked under the bed and checked her closet, too, even poking through the dirty laundry in her laundry bag. Now you're starting to act crazy, she scolded herself. There was no way the music could have gotten mixed up with the laundry.

Some people mislaid things all the time, but

Hope wasn't one of them. She distinctly remembered putting the music inside the purple case that she used to carry the rest of her orchestra music and her school papers. Or, at least, she thought she remembered. The more she tried to recall exactly what she had done on Tuesday afternoon, the more confused she felt. Maybe Mr. Martin had been right after all. Maybe she was trying to cram too many activities into her days.

She was just about to give up and get undressed for the evening when she heard voices in the living room and then her mother knocking on her bedroom door. "Hope, dear, you have a visitor," Mrs. Chang said in a low voice.

"Who is it?" she asked. "Is it Peter?"

Caroline Chang shook her head. "It's Sean Dubrow." There was a hint of disapproval in her voice. She didn't care for the idea of her daughter having an uninvited visitor at ten o'clock at night.

"I'll see what he wants," Hope said. "It's probably just some message about cheerleading."

When Hope entered the living room, Sean couldn't help thinking what a contrast she was to the flashy Diana Tucker. Even though she was wearing jeans and a T-shirt Hope was the picture of neatness. Her shiny, blunt-cut hair looked freshly combed, not a strand out of place. Her jeans were meticulously ironed. Her pink T-shirt had little cap sleeves that gave it a feminine look.

Sean vaguely realized that some people wouldn't think it was right for him to be moving in on a girl who had just that day broken up with her boyfriend. But that wasn't the way he looked at it. Hope needed comfort, and who could be better at giving it than he was? Still, there was something about Hope that made Sean nervous. She was so straightforward, so perfect. And it wasn't an act, either. Hope Chang was exactly what she seemed to be.

"I just stopped by because I was wondering how you were feeling," he said uneasily.

"Feeling?" Hope looked confused. "I'm fine. Why?"

"Well, I know things like this can be tough. I've been there myself. Lots of times, actually."

Hope assumed Sean had heard the story of her lost sheet music, though she wasn't sure why Sean should be so concerned. "It's just that I feel like such a klutz," she said. "Like my life is out of control."

"It isn't the end of the world. You can still go out with just about any guy you want." He flashed his best heartbreaker of a smile. "Like me, for instance."

Now she was completely puzzled. "Go out? What does losing my sheet music have to do with going out? Am I going crazy, or is everyone else?"

"Sheet music! I was talking about Peter," said Sean.

"Peter? What about him?"

Belatedly it dawned on him that Hope hadn't heard anything about Peter and Diana. He took an automatic step backward, wondering how he was going to get out of this one. Maybe the safest thing would be just to bolt for the door without saying another word.

But Hope wasn't going to let him get away without an explanation. Drawing herself up to her full five feet four inches, she stepped between Sean and the door, blocking his escape route. "Sean Dubrow, you tell me this instant what this is all about," she demanded.

"It's probably all a big misunderstanding," he said quickly. "I was talking to Diana at Pineland Spa, and I thought she said that she and Peter were going steady. I must have heard wrong."

"I guess you must have." Hope looked grim. "Or else Diana is living in some kind of fantasy world."

As soon as Sean left, Hope went to the phone to call Peter. Part of her was sure that Diana was lying. But another part of her had a premonition that she had been betrayed.

"Peter, I've got to know," she said, as soon as he was on the line. "Is it true about you and Diana?"

"Uh, is what true?"

"If you have to ask, that means there is something going on. Sean just told me that Diana says the two of you are going steady."

"What!" Peter was outraged. "No way!"

"She must have some reason for saying that."

"Honest, Hope, she doesn't," Peter protested. "We just spent last evening together, that's all. And only because she was feeling low and needed someone to talk to."

"You went out with her? Where?"

Peter swallowed hard, "Well, actually, we

ended up at Chez Marcel. But that was kind of an accident."

"Peter, no one ends up at Chez Marcel by accident. It isn't the 7-Eleven. It's the fanciest restaurant in the county!"

She didn't wait for him to come up with an explanation. She'd heard enough, and for once, she impolitely hung up the phone while someone was still talking.

She was headed back to her room when Mrs. Chang stuck her head out of her studio and said pleasantly, "I hope Sean's visit at least got your mind off whatever it was that was bothering you."

"Oh, it did," she assured her mother. "You can bet it did."

There would be no more looking for the music that evening. Hope slammed the door to her room behind her and sprawled on her bed, trying her best to choke back her tears. It was bad enough that Peter no longer cared for her, but why couldn't he at least have been honest enough to tell her what was going on? How was she ever going to face her friends at school tomorrow? And worst of all, how was she going to manage to face having to be with Peter at cheerleading practice?

CHAPTER

 10

"You're looking pale, dear, so I fixed you a nice, nourishing breakfast." Mrs. Evans plunked down a steaming bowl of oatmeal on the table. Olivia took one whiff of it and winced. Why her mother thought of oatmeal as an all-purpose remedy was something she never would understand. Fortunately, she was perfectly healthy or the mere smell of the stuff would probably have sent her to bed for the rest of the day.

But she had finally learned that there was no point in trying to argue her mom out of her strange ideas. Doing her best to look appreciative, she managed to get down a few bites. "Thanks for going to all the effort," she said, pushing the half-filled bowl away. "But you shouldn't have given me so much. It's so filling."

"Well, at least you ate a little, dear. It will do you good."

With that, Mrs. Evans left the room in confusion. She was so used to Olivia's protestations that she hadn't quite figured out how to deal with her daughter's new, agreeable nature.

Without being asked, Olivia stacked the breakfast dishes in the dishwasher and cleaned off the table. Tact had its uses. She wondered nervously whether tact would also work when it came to dealing with Holly Hudson.

Olivia took the bus to school and hurried to Holly's locker, to be sure to catch her before homeroom. She'd gone over what she planned to say a hundred times. If Holly would give up her idea of emceeing the pep rally, then she would be willing to compromise on the card stunts.

It didn't make sense for the captain of the cheerleaders and the president of the Pompon Squad to be barely speaking to each other. Holly was sure to see that, once Olivia offered to make peace. Even though she had her faults, Holly was sincere about wanting the team to have the whole school behind its efforts.

Holly showed up at her locker about two minutes before the late bell was due to ring. She did not look as if she was in a good mood. Olivia saw her plans for a nice, civilized discussion falling apart. But it was too late now to escape.

"What do you want?" Holly challenged her. "I suppose you came to gloat."

"I don't know what you're talking about," Olivia said in all innocence. "I thought we ought to get together and discuss tomorrow's rally. It's silly for us to be arguing about it. I'm sorry if you thought I was unreasonable before. I mean, everyone knows what you've made of the Pompon Squad."

Holly slammed shut the door of her locker with a bang. "I knew it! You did come to gloat. You really are one spiteful girl, Olivia Evans. For that matter, I bet you set the whole thing up. Just you wait, I'll find a way to get even."

With that, Holly departed, chewing fast and furiously on a stick of gum.

It wasn't until after first period, when Olivia heard about the Pompon Squad mutiny from Bobbie Reynolds, that she started to figure out why Holly had been so angry.

"You just picked a bad time to compliment Holly on her handling of the squad," Bobbie commiserated. "The way things look now I'm not even sure there is a squad anymore. We could sell popcorn all over the state and there still wouldn't be enough money in the treasury to buy jackets for everyone who showed up at that meeting. Unfortunately, the freshmen and sophomores don't understand that. The rumor got around, and now that it turns out not to be true, they blame Holly."

Olivia couldn't think of anything that she could do about the situation. Holly's pushiness had been a problem. But if the Pompon Squad fell apart that would be worse still.

Olivia loved cheering. There was no greater thrill than being out there on the gym floor, and knowing that you were responsible for building the crowd's excitement and fighting spirit. The rest of the headaches that went with the job were a different story. She had no idea what, if anything, she could do to save the situation.

Before practice that afternoon she went to see Coach Engborg, who was no help at all. "Holly got herself into this mess," the coach said. "And I still think she deserves a chance to work it out."

"But what about tomorrow's rally?" Olivia wailed. "We were counting on the Pompon Squad to present a skit, and I'm sure with all this arguing they didn't get around to planning anything. What's going to happen?"

Ardith Engborg looked pained. "Why ask me? You're the one who keeps saying that emceeing the rally is the cheerleading squad captain's job."

As she changed to get ready for practice, Olivia found herself thinking about a saying that Duffy always referred to as Murphy's Law: Everything that can go wrong, will go wrong.

That was certainly true where this rally was concerned. At least now I know we've hit bottom, she consoled herself. Nothing could be worse than this.

But she was wrong about that, too.

The new routine that the cheerleading squad had been working up was based mostly on three-person stunts. Sean worked with the taller girls, Tara and Jessica, while Peter Rayman teamed up with Hope and Olivia. Today, however, as soon as the warm-ups were over, Hope quietly but firmly announced that she did not want to be in Peter's group.

"But you've got to," Olivia told her. "Otherwise the proportions will be all wrong."

"I'm sorry about that," Hope said. "But I just can't. Not today."

Peter looked as stunned as the rest of them. "What's this all about?" he asked in bewilderment. "You didn't say anything to me about this."

Hope was the picture of injured pride. "You didn't bother to tell me you went out with Diana Tucker, either."

"How did you find out about that, anyway?" Peter blurted out. He looked at Jessica, who just shook her head. Then at Sean, who was suddenly very busy counting the tiles in the gym ceiling.

Peter knew a guilty expression when he saw one. After all, he was wearing one himself. "You!" he barked at Sean. "You're the last person who ought to be spreading stories about other people."

"Don't blame me for your problems," Sean said indignantly. "Diana didn't mention anything about it being a secret."

At the mention of Diana's name, Hope looked as if she was about to burst into tears.

How would Mary Ellen have handled this? Olivia asked herself. For once, though, she was too angry to worry about the answer. "You can finish this argument after practice," she snapped. "For now, we're going to put our personal problems aside and do the routine the way it was choreographed."

To her astonishment, everyone did just that.

Even Hope didn't protest when Peter put his arm around her waist to lift her into a side stag, although she didn't look happy, either. No one could say that the rest of the practice went well, but at least it went relatively smoothly. Hope didn't say another word for the rest of the session, and when it was over she changed in record time and slipped out of the locker room through the fire exit door.

The other girls watched her go, feeling sympathetic but helpless. "I can't figure that girl out," Tara said as the door slammed behind Hope. "You'd think she'd want someone to confide in when she's so unhappy. Doesn't she trust us?"

Jessica bit her lip. "I guess I can't blame her if she doesn't trust me right now. Patrick and I saw Peter and Diana together. I didn't know what to do, so I didn't say anything." Silently, she wondered if her friends would do the same if they happened to know something about Patrick getting back together with Mary Ellen. That was the trouble with jealousy — you could never be sure that the people you trusted most weren't also keeping secrets from you.

"I know just how Hope feels," Olivia put in. "When I feel upset, sometimes I just need to be alone."

That's for sure, thought Tara. For the last week she'd been making a special effort to be friendly to Olivia, and so far she'd seen no sign that Olivia had even noticed. For that matter, getting a car sure hadn't done anything to improve her social life, either. It didn't seem fair that people like Hope and Olivia, who preferred to be left alone, got all the sympathy.

Tara took her time getting dressed, putting off the moment when she'd have to arrive home for another boring evening of homework and TV. She dawdled in front the mirror so long that Coach Engborg finally called into the locker room to ask if everything was okay.

"No problem," Tara shouted back. "I'll be out in a sec."

Hurrying now, she gathered up her things and waved goodbye to the coach, who was sitting in her office making some phone calls. The hall outside the gym was deserted. Normally, there were at least a few after-school activities that ran overtime, but tonight it seemed that everyone but she had been in a hurry to clear out. She was wearing her brown suede boots with cleats on the heels, and the tapping sound they made as she walked echoed through the empty corridor. Some of the classrooms on the main floor had already been cleaned and the lights turned off.

The quiet was so complete it was almost spooky. It was like one of those movies, Tara thought, where the heroine suddenly wakes up to find that civilization has been destroyed and she's the last human being left on Earth.

But as she was scolding herself for being nervous, she noticed a long, menacing shadow ahead of her, just beyond the place where the hallway joined the main lobby. Someone — or something — was standing just beyond the doorway. Tara froze in her tracks. She wasn't scared enough to turn around and detour all the way back to one of the side entrances. On the other hand, she wanted to check out that shadow before whoever was casting it had a chance to see her first. Gathering her courage, she tiptoed the last fifteen feet in silence. Her umbrella was firmly clutched in her right hand, ready to be used as a weapon if necessary. Reaching the door, she peered cautiously around the corner . . . and found herself face-to-face with a very large, frizzy mop, standing on end in an oversized scrub bucket.

"BOO!"

The voice was deep and resonant but definitely one hundred percent human. Tara wheeled around and saw Kirby Hopkins, the boy who sat behind her in English class, standing across the lobby beside the pay telephone. He was leaning against the wall, arms folded across his chest and an amused grin plastered across his handsome, square-jawed face.

"I hope you're pleased with yourself, Kirby," she huffed. "You scared me half to death."

"You mean the mop did," Kirby laughed. "I'm sorry, but I couldn't resist. You were quite a sight, slinking down the hall like that."

Tara's dark eyes flashed. "I wasn't slinking. I was just being careful."

"Probably a good idea at that," he said. "You never know when you're going to find an unsavory character like me hanging around in the lobby."

Tara couldn't help smiling at this. Kirby Hopkins was easily the most clean-cut-looking guy in the senior class. His hair was red, but of a lighter shade than Tara's, and his eyes were a startling china blue. His muscular arms were covered with freckles.

"Seriously, I need to borrow a quarter, if you can spare one," Kirby said. "I was supposed to be playing tennis over at the junior college courts, but the fellow I usually play with canceled at the last minute. In the meantime, I missed the last bus home, and when I tried to call my folks for a ride, the phone ate the only change I had and then disconnected me. I guess it just isn't my lucky day."

That's right, thought Tara. Kirby Hopkins doesn't have a car. That was probably the reason why she'd never paid any serious attention to him before. Tara knew she was something of a snob when it came to the subject of cars, but she just couldn't see herself taking the bus on a date. Or, worse yet, being chauffeured around by some guy's parents.

Suddenly, it occurred to her that it didn't make such a big difference anymore whether her dates had their own cars or not. She had the Chevy, didn't she? She wondered whether she should offer Kirby a lift to the tennis courts. Would he think she was coming on to him?

She decided it was worth the risk. "The college isn't too far out of my way," she lied. "If you still want to go over there I could drop you off."

"Gee, thanks, but there isn't much point since I don't have a partner." Kirby brightened. "I don't suppose you play tennis?"

104

"I do, but I don't have a racquet."

"That's okay. We can borrow one from my buddy's locker."

Tara made a quick call home, and five minutes later they were in the Chevy, heading for the tennis courts.

"Nice car," Kirby said admiringly. His eyes fastened on the tiny gold-tone charm with the word "Velvet" on it that Tara had bought and fastened to her precious car keys. "What does that mean?" he asked.

"Oh, nothing special. It's just a nickname I gave the car."

"As in *National Velvet*?"

Tara was surprised. "I thought only girls read that book. How come you know about it?"

Kirby looked slightly embarrassed. "My big sister used to read to me. Don't tell anybody, okay?"

Tara smiled. "Okay. It'll be our secret." She wasn't intrigued with Kirby in a big way, but they were getting along better than she'd expected.

Tara was an excellent tennis player. She had taken lessons at summer camp for years, but seldom played in Tarenton because her friends weren't good enough to give her any real competition. Kirby's serve was a good deal more powerful than hers, but Tara was quicker on her feet, and once they started volleying, they were more or less evenly matched.

"I can't believe it!" Kirby exclaimed after they'd split two hard-fought sets. "You're a terrific player, and I never so much as heard that you knew the game. I thought — " He stopped abruptly.

"What did you think?" Tara pressed.

Kirby gave her an apologetic smile. "Basically, that you were all flash and no substance. But I'm the first to admit I was wrong."

That, unfortunately, was the story of Tara's life. Other girls envied her long, coppery hair and curvaceous figure. But Tara was convinced that her attention-getting looks were a liability. Not that she wanted to be ugly. Looking good was important to her. Still, she often wished that she could change places with green-eyed, winsome Jessica or petite, dark-eyed Hope. Neither of them had the kind of looks that scared people away.

"I know that 'beautiful but dumb' is a stereotype," Kirby said, reading her mind. "But the last girl I played tennis with was Diana Tucker, and believe me, she fit the image perfectly."

"You played tennis with Diana?" for a newcomer, that girl certainly did get around, Tara thought.

"I ran into her during her first day at school," Kirby explained, "and she went on about how she had been on the tennis team at her school back in California. So it seemed natural to ask her to play a few sets on Saturday. She's so great-looking I admit my mind wasn't totally on the game. But it turned out to be a disaster I wouldn't want to repeat."

"A disaster? What do you mean?"

Kirby shook his head. "Take my word for it, Diana Tucker never played on any tennis team anywhere."

"But wasn't she awfully embarrassed about having lied?"

"Not as much as I was," Kirby said. "That was the strange part. My guess is that she tells so many lies that she half believes them herself. When it became obvious that she was a lousy player, she tried to blame her performance on a pulled muscle. I knew that wasn't the problem. I mean, she barely knew how to keep score."

CHAPTER

When Tara got home she found the house empty. Her parents had gone out to a dinner party and Marie had gone for the night. There was a casserole in the refrigerator that only needed to be heated up, but she wasn't in the mood to eat. Instead she poured herself a big glass of orange juice and sat down to think over the afternoon's developments.

First of all, there was Kirby. Did she like him as a friend, or was there more to her feelings than that? And what would happen if she did want to date him? Since she had a car and he didn't, did that mean that it would be up to her to ask him out next time?

Tara didn't see anything wrong with asking a guy out, especially one who was as nice as Kirby. Other girls did it, she knew. But if Tara Armstrong asked a boy for a date, it would be sure to be the talk of the school in no time.

And for all she knew, Kirby might turn her down. Maybe he'd be embarrassed by the idea of going out on a real date with a girl who did the driving. If he said no, she'd be completely mortified.

Unable to decide what to do about Kirby, Tara turned her thoughts to Diana Tucker. She'd been suspicious of Diana from the beginning, but Kirby had given her proof that Diana was a fraud. If she lied about being a good tennis player, then she was probably lying about having been a cheerleader, too. No doubt all the stories she'd been telling Holly about being able to get the Pompon Squad custom-designed jackets was another fantasy. And if Diana had been out with Kirby over the weekend, that made it even more unlikely that she really cared about Peter Rayman.

It especially bothered her that sensible Kirby Hopkins had assumed that she and Diana were the same type. The more she thought about that, the angrier she got.

Acting on impulse, Tara called information and got Diana Tucker's phone number. She called, and the impersonal voice of a maid gave her the Tuckers' address, just down the road from her own house. If Tara left right away, it was still not too late in the evening for Diana to receive a surprise visit from a new neighbor.

Five minutes later, Tara found herself banging on the Tuckers' polished oak front door. Her knock was answered by Mrs. Tucker, a stylishly thin, unhappy-looking woman dressed in a black hostess gown.

"Isn't this nice. I'm always happy to meet one of Diana's friends," Mrs. Tucker enthused, in a voice that suggested that she hadn't met very many of them up until now.

She was so pleased that Tara started to feel guilty. Then Diana slouched into the room, wearing white sweat pants, a turquoise turtleneck, and a sour scowl. "What is this? The welcome wagon?" she asked, suspiciously.

Mrs. Tucker, looking completely cowed, retreated from the room without another word.

"Not exactly," Tara said angrily. "I just thought it was time that the two of us had a little talk. I know exactly what you've been doing to make trouble for the cheerleading squad and for Holly, and I don't like it."

Calmly, Tara accused Diana of pretending to be Holly's friend while she was really doing everything possible to break up the Pompon Squad.

Diana did not look very repentant. "What if it's true?" she asked in a bored voice. "You can't prove that. Besides, there's no law against giving people ideas. I can't help it if Holly was dumb enough to listen to me."

"You're even lower than I thought," Tara returned. "I might be able to understand your coming between Peter and Hope if you really cared about him. But you don't at all. That was just another of your little ploys for hurting the cheerleading squad."

"Are you finished?"

"No, I'm not. I'm not going until you at least admit that you stole Peter from Hope out of jealousy. For that matter, I bet you're the one who stole Hope's music, too."

Tara had just thrown that last accusation on impulse, but the scared look on Diana's face told her she had hit on the truth. "There *is* a law against stealing, last I heard," she finished triumphantly.

"Okay. You win," Diana said defiantly. "What do you want from me?"

"For starters, you can stop making trouble for the cheerleaders," Tara told her. "And you can tell Peter the real reason you were chasing him."

Diana looked as if she were struggling not to scream or burst into tears. "You must think I'm a terrible person," she blurted out at last. "But it isn't easy moving around all the time, always being the new girl in town. Just because I can spend money for clothes and live in a fancy house, people assume I'm some kind of snob. So why shouldn't I act that way? And why shouldn't I be jealous of Hope? And of Olivia and Holly, too? I'll never be elected captain or president of anything."

"Those are just excuses," Tara snapped. "Stop feeling sorry for yourself."

But the excuses had a familiar ring to them. She sometimes had similar feelings.

"You've got to give me some time to straighten things out," Diana pressed on. "I can't just call up Peter and tell him I never cared about him at all.

That would be cruel. Besides, it isn't even true. I do like him — I think he's sort of cute."

"Okay," Tara conceded. "But you'd better do it soon. And in the meantime, see that Hope gets her music back."

I'd better get out of here before I give in and let Diana off the hook completely, Tara warned herself. She was used to being the one who was accused of selfishness. Indignation didn't come that easily to her. Besides, she couldn't *really* prove that Diana had done anything wrong. Fortunately, Diana hadn't figured that out yet.

"I'll make a deal with you," Tara said aloud. "I won't turn you in for taking the music as long as Hope gets it back. But you'd better talk to Peter before Saturday night."

There was a game with Deep River on Saturday evening, and Tara figured that Peter and Hope could use the occasion to make up.

In the meantime, there was tomorrow afternoon's pep rally to consider. After leaving the Tucker house, Tara drove down to the Pancake House in Tarenton and phoned Holly and Olivia with the same message: "I have something really important to talk over," she told each of them. "Can you meet me here in five minutes?"

Both girls lived nearby, and they were both curious enough to wonder what mysterious news Tara might have to confide to them.

Holly arrived first, breathless with excitement. She loved gossip and being in the center of exciting new developments. "What's the big mystery?" she asked gleefully.

"You'll see in a minute," Tara told her.

Right on cue, Olivia walked in the door. She and Holly stared at each other in surprise.

"You're probably wondering why I called you all together," Tara said, attempting a joke. It fell flat, but at least Olivia didn't bolt out the door.

"I just thought it was time for the two of you to sit down and do some planning for tomorrow's rally," Tara told them. "I can't do it. No one can, except you. And I figured that you'd be willing to stop quarreling and cooperate if you just had a chance."

If Olivia was surprised at Tara's role of peacemaker, she didn't show it. She knew common sense when she heard it. "I'm ready for a truce if you are," she told Holly.

Holly hesitated for just a second, then decided that she couldn't afford to walk out on Olivia's offer. "Fine," she said, sitting down at the table with the others. "I even have an idea for a skit. Maybe the two of you can help me work it out."

The next day at lunch, the other members of the cheerleading squad and the Pompon Squad officers held a lunchtime meeting to hear about the plans for the skit.

"Talk about typecasting!" Sean exclaimed when he heard about the starring role he was to play. The skit was a takeoff on the story of *Little Red Riding Hood*, and he, naturally, was going to play the wolf. And he wasn't too happy about having to wear the old wolf mascot suit, a shabby, fake-fur outfit that had seen better days. But being the star was worth the inconvenience.

Andy Poletti was less than thrilled with his assignment, too. Wearing a ridiculous blond wig, tights, and a jumper, he was going to be cast as Little Red Riding Hood.

"Why me?" Andy groused when Holly explained the idea of the skit.

Soon, however, Holly, Carla Simpson, and the others talked Andy into going along with the idea. "Everybody likes you," Holly pointed out. "And besides, there's no time to write out a script. You'll know how to ad-lib. You're just a naturally funny person, Andy. People take one look at you and they're ready to laugh."

"That isn't exactly a compliment," Andy complained. But he was smiling as he said it, because he knew there was some truth to what Holly said. If anybody could pull off her idea, he was the one for the job.

CHAPTER

12

The rally got underway with the whole squad except for Sean leading the student body in the school song and a few warm up cheers. Then Olivia announced the cheer that was going to be the cue for Sean's entrance.

"Our team is red hot," she screamed.
"Their team is all shot. . . ."

The last lines of the cheer were gradually drowned in the tide of laughter that began when the students noticed Sean, lounging at the side of the stage in his wolf outfit. He had been wearing the wolf's head when he first appeared, but at the last minute he had realized that no one had bothered to wonder how he could say his lines with the head on. Undaunted, he removed the head and held it under his arm, then began leering in a convincing wolflike fashion at a group of giggly freshmen girls in the front row.

Over his wolf suit, Sean was wearing a red windbreaker jacket. As soon as he had everyone's attention, he turned around to model the back of the jacket, giving the audience a chance to see the white felt letters that Betsey and Carla had hastily sewn across the back: POMPON SQUAD.

The laughter died down and there was a good deal of anxious whispering. By now, everyone in school had an opinion on the jacket question, and quite a few kids didn't find the subject the least bit funny.

Then Andy Poletti appeared at the other side of the stage, skipping along in his Little Red Riding Hood costume, and the wave of laughter started all over again. Andy was like no Little Red Riding Hood the world had ever seen before. Instead of acting scared and shy, he greeted Sean with a bold, "Hey there, Mr. Wolf. I know this great club. It's called Grandma's Place. Want to go dancing?"

Grinning at the audience, Andy confided, "If I can get this wolf to ask me to go steady, maybe he'll give me his jacket to wear."

The wolf looked more and more nervous as Andy backed him into a corner. "What pearly teeth you have, Mr. Wolf," he leered. "What bee-yoo-ti-ful eyes. . . . And what a nice jacket! . . . It's so much nicer than this old riding hood I've been wearing around."

When Sean finally panicked and tried to run,

Andy reached out and took hold of the back of the jacket to stop him. Soon the two of them were tussling on the floor of the stage, each pulling on one sleeve of the jacket in a slapstick tug of war.

Now it was time for Olivia to play her part. Wading into the fight, she pulled the two of them apart. "Aren't you two ashamed of yourselves?" she exclaimed in mock anger, "Fighting over a jacket, when you should be thinking about promoting school spirit. Why don't you get your priorities straight?"

Andy and Sean both looked abashed. "I guess you're right," they said in unison, "there are more important things."

"That's right!" shouted Tara, Jessica, Hope, and Peter, joining the others on centerstage. "Let's get behind the team."

"From now on, I promise to be good," said Sean, with a mischievous expression that brought down the house.

Olivia could tell from the good-natured laughter that was mixed in with applause that the skit had been a success. Sean and Andy had managed to make the whole fight over the jackets look silly. They had even gotten the students who were upset about it to start laughing at themselves.

"We hope you Pompon Squad members won't mind that we've had a few laughs with our little skit," Olivia said into the microphone. "We cheerleaders really appreciate you, and we want to thank you for all the support you've given us."

There was applause and a few scattered cheers.

"Maybe some of you don't realize it, but the

Pompon Squad raised over three hundred dollars last year for charity. And that's besides the money they gave to the athletics fund. Good work, guys."

There was more applause, louder this time. Holly and the other officers, seated in the front row of the auditorium, beamed with pride.

Tara, from her place on stage, searched out Diana and located her sitting a few rows behind the Pompon Squad leaders. The sulky look on Diana's face said that she was not happy at all. That's one little scheme of hers foiled, Tara assured herself.

After Olivia's speech, the rest of the rally went smoothly. When the cheerleaders swung into their new pompon routine to the tune of "Alexander's Ragtime Band," the entire Pompon Squad section sang along, reading the lyrics Holly and Olivia had written from Xeroxed sheets.

> "We are the wolves,
> The big bad wolves,
> We're the baddest team around!
> Just watch us prowl,
> Just hear us growl,
> We're the baddest team in town!
> When the wolves are on the move,
> Other teams run and hide,
> We are the wolves from Tarenton. . . .
> You bet we are!"

Inspired by the singing, the cheerleaders performed flawlessly, executing crisp high jumps and kicks that were far better than anything they'd done in practice.

Even Hope looked as if she was enjoying herself. No one in the audience could have guessed that her carefree smile was anything but genuine. And for once even Olivia was fooled.

Peter Rayman, who was still teamed up with the reluctant Hope for the partner lifts, knew better. When he put his hands around Hope's waist to raise her into the butterfly lift, he could feel her imperceptibly shrinking under his touch. Her whole body seemed to be vibrating with tension.

Peter was amazed. Ever since she'd confronted him at practice, Hope had been cold but controlled. He knew she was angry with him for lying. Peter himself had been torn by conflicting emotions all week long. But because he didn't think that guys were supposed to show their feelings, he'd done a fairly good job of acting unconcerned. Still, it hadn't occurred to him that Hope had been putting on an act of her own. Hope was so disciplined, so quiet, that it was easy to forget how vulnerable she was.

As the lift ended and Peter gently set Hope down, their eyes met for the first time since the routine began. The eye contact lasted only a few seconds, but that was long enough for Peter to get the message. There was more than hurt pride behind Hope's outburst the previous day. She still cared about him.

Peter went through the last few minutes of the

rally in a daze. If only he could get Hope alone and tell her how he really felt, he was sure they could work everything out. Unfortunately, when the last cheer of the day ended, Peter was at the far end of the line, standing next to Jessica and Tara.

"Wasn't that a great rally?" Jessica said enthusiastically as the last chords of the fight song died out and the audience started to leave. "Didn't Sean make a great wolf?"

"Terrific," Peter agreed. But his attention was focused on Hope, who was moving quickly and deliberately in the direction of the girl's locker room. Once she disappeared inside, she would probably manage to avoid him again by slipping out the side exit. He had to get to her before she could escape.

"Excuse me," he told Jessica hastily. He started off in Hope's direction, his heart pounding as he saw that she had turned around and was half waiting for him to catch up with her.

Then, suddenly, he felt Diana Tucker's dragonlady fingernails clamp shut around his left arm. "Peter!" she squealed, planting a proprietary kiss on his cheek. "That was really something, seeing you in action like that. You're even stronger than I thought."

Peter saw the soft expression on Hope's face harden instantly. "Talk to you later," he told Diana. But it was too late. By the time he crossed the gym, Hope had already vanished through the door to the locker room.

Diana, meanwhile, did not show any signs of

having noticed that she was getting the brush-off. "I'll meet you in the parking lot in ten minutes," she told him. "My folks aren't home for once, so I thought we could listen to records and, you know, spend some time alone together."

Peter hesitated. He didn't much like Diana, and he certainly didn't care for her possessive ways. But she was still a great-looking girl. And Hope wasn't giving him a fair chance. If she couldn't trust him more than she did, they weren't ever going to work things out.

"Okay," he told Diana. "I'll meet you as soon as I change clothes."

Hope spent a long time in the shower, trying to compose herself. By the time she emerged it was impossible to tell whether her eyes were puffy from crying or just from the steaming hot water. As she stood under one of the wall-mounted hair dryers, the other girls studied her for signs of emotion.

"Are you all right?" Jessica asked timidly.

"Of course I am," Hope said.

Jessica, who had noticed Hope watching the scene between Peter and Diana, was not convinced. "I don't want to pry," she said, "but if you need someone to talk to, I'm available. I know how it feels. . . ."

Hope squared her small, determined shoulders and turned away. She had been brought up to believe that it was very important to keep her feelings under control. Even though she knew Jessica meant well, it almost seemed that she was purposely trying to prod her into bursting into tears and making a fool of herself.

"Oh, I'm okay," she said, doing her best to sound cheerful. "It's probably for the best that Peter is interested in someone else. I'm too busy to date, anyway. So I've been saved having to hurt Peter's feelings."

"So everything worked out for the best?" Jessica asked doubtfully. She was sure Hope was just trying to cover her feelings, but Tara joined them before she could say any more.

"I was just wondering," Tara asked Hope. "Did you ever find that sheet music you lost?"

Hope brightened immediately. And this time there was no doubt that her smile was genuine. "It was the craziest thing," she told Tara. "When I went into the orchestra room this morning, there it was, sitting on one of the music stands. I'm sure I searched that room from top to bottom on Wednesday and it wasn't there."

"That's funny," said Jessica. "What do you think happened?"

Hope shrugged. "Maybe somebody picked it up by mistake and then returned it when they realized it wasn't theirs. Although it's hard to see how that could happen. The cover is a different color from any of the pieces the orchestra is using.

"Anyway," she went on, "I don't really care what happened as long as the music was found. Now I don't have to face Mr. Martin, and it still isn't too late for me to catch up on my practicing."

"That's great!" Tara was beaming with pleasure. "I'm sure everything is going to work out for you," she assured Hope. "Don't be discouraged. You just wait and see."

Jessica shot Tara a suspicious look. It almost seemed as if she were taking credit for the reappearance of Hope's music! There was something funny about the way Tara had been acting all day. She just hoped that it wouldn't lead to trouble.

CHAPTER

When Tara woke up on Saturday morning she found that it had snowed overnight. Hugging her cream-colored satin bathrobe around her, she ran to her bedroom window and looked out. Only an inch or so of new snow had fallen, just enough to make the landscape look fresh and sparkling.

This would be a perfect day for an ice-skating party, she thought. The day was crisp and clear, and there hadn't been enough snow to cover the ice on the ponds. She thought longingly of her favorite ice-skating spot, a place called Grover's Pond about fifteen miles out of town.

Unfortunately, she only got there a few times every winter. Tarenton was so far north that most kids in town grew up knowing how to ice-skate, but by the time they got into high school a lot of them had lost interest. Tara still loved skating as much as ever, but recently, she hadn't known anyone who was interested in going with her.

Then the bright idea struck. What a dummy I am! she thought. I have a car of my own. I don't need to wait to be invited.

Tara ran downstairs and fixed herself a breakfast of cereal with sliced bananas and a mug of tea with hot milk. By the time Tara had finished eating, her plans for the day had become grander than ever. The squad deserved some fun after working so hard to bring off yesterday's pep rally. Why shouldn't she invite them all to come along with her?

Her hardest decision was whether or not to invite Peter. Peter was by far the best skater on the squad, almost good enough to be a competitive figure skater. But, of course, he and Hope weren't exactly in the mood to party together. Tara decided to take a chance and call him anyway. She couldn't help hoping that Diana would have had her talk with Peter already. If so, today's party could be just the occasion for he and Hope to make up.

But Peter's reaction to the invitation squelched that idea. "Thanks, Tara," he said glumly. "But I'm just not in the mood."

"Did something happen between you and Diana?" Tara couldn't resist asking.

"I'd rather not talk about it. I just think I'll give Hope a break and stay out of her way, at least until the game tonight."

Tara assumed that meant that Diana *had* told Peter that there was no future in their relationship. Otherwise, why would he sound so glum? "Don't take it too hard," she advised. "I'm sure you'll be feeling better by this evening."

Peter hung up the phone and shook his head. He was sure that Tara was referring to his quarrel with Hope, but he couldn't figure out why he was supposed to feel better by this evening.

Actually, Peter had no plans at all for feeling better any time soon. He still felt lousy about the way he had treated Hope, and his date with Diana the previous evening had been so weird that he was still trying to figure out what had happened.

First of all, when he met Diana in the parking lot after the rally, she had been out of breath and acting very mysterious. He never had figured out what about. Then, almost as soon as they got to the Tucker house, Diana had kissed him. Not that he minded having physical contact with Diana. In fact, that was practically all he'd been thinking about for the past week.

Somehow every time he tried to sort out his feelings about Diana his mind reeled in confusion. Being kissed by her after the rally in front of half the school had been a tremendous boost to his ego. And seeing her look at him as if he were the sexiest guy in school did even more for his pride. So why wasn't he having any fun?

Missing Tara's skating party, just because he couldn't bring himself to face Hope, was just about the final straw. As he settled down for a dull afternoon of catching up on his homework, he found himself trying to figure out just what Diana was up to. She certainly had been in a strange mood last evening, even for her.

The rest of Tara's calls were more successful.

Jessica Bennett had just heard that Patrick was going to be working yet another Saturday, and she was happy to have a chance to get out and enjoy herself.

Olivia was more or less in the same boat, having just learned that Duffy was supposed to cover a bowling tournament at Pinelands Mall Lanes for his newspaper. "Duffy said I should come along," she told Tara, "but watching a lot of strangers bowl isn't my idea of a good time. I'd much rather come skating."

Hope said no at first, but then changed her mind and agreed to come along when she heard that Peter wasn't going to be in the group. She had been so tense all week long, and a day of relaxation was just what she needed.

Sean also turned Tara down at first. "I'm supposed to have a new radio put in my car," he told her.

"You don't need to hang around and supervise them while they install it, do you?" Tara kidded him, knowing that this was probably exactly what Sean had planned. "Why don't you drop off your car, and you can come with us in the Chevy?"

"Okay," Sean agreed. "If you think we can all fit into one car."

There was plenty of room in the car for five people, even dressed for skating, but waiting for Sean to leave his Fiero at the garage meant that it was well after noon by the time Tara picked him up. Then she had to make the rounds of the other kids' houses.

On the way out to Grover's Pond, Olivia kept checking her watch. "Are you sure we have time for this?" she asked anxiously. "Tonight's game starts at six-thirty."

Sean laughed. "Don't be such a worrier. There's plenty of time."

When they arrived at the pond, they were delighted to find that the ice wasn't crowded as it sometimes got on Saturdays. There were two couples, strangers who must have come from the junior college at Hillsborough, and a father who was trying to teach his three children to skate.

Jessica got her skates on first and did a few fast turns around the perimeter of the pond. "The ice is perfect," she called out as she skated by.

Sean, meanwhile, volunteered to give a quick lesson to Hope. Although she could barely totter along on her skates, Hope looked chic, as usual. Unlike the other girls, who were in pants, she had on a short gray skating skirt, which she was wearing with pink tights and her pink and gray down vest. "Wouldn't you know," Tara said, watching their progress. "Hope can hardly skate but she's still the only one of us with the correct clothes."

"Oh, who cares?" said Olivia. "I'm going to see if Jessica can show me how to do a spin."

Tara finished lacing up her skates and skated alone around the ice. Even though she was wearing jeans instead of a little flared skirt like Hope's, she knew she looked good. She had on a new sweater, and her matching legwarmers of multi-colored rainbow yarn ran the spectrum from deep indigo to yellow.

The day was perfect — or almost perfect. If only I had someone to skate with, a real date, Tara thought.

As if on cue, another skater came up behind her, then did a fast turn so that he was skating backward a few feet in front of her. "Is this a cheerleader's party, or can I join in?" he asked.

"Kirby! What are you doing here?"

Kirby let loose one of his barrel-chested laughs. "Does that mean I'm welcome or not?"

"Of course!" On second thought, Tara was afraid of sounding too eager, so she added, "It's a free pond, after all."

But she was wasting her time trying to strike the right note of welcome. Kirby wasn't much interested in conversation, flirtatious or otherwise. "Want to skate over to the other side of the pond?" he asked.

Tara nodded and they took off, moving side by side at a good pace. Despite its name, Grover's Pond covered several acres, and soon they had left the other skaters behind.

"Do you know how to waltz on skates?" Kirby asked.

"Sure, but there's no music," Tara said.

"Not so." Kirby showed her the pocket-sized sports radio he was carrying in his jacket pocket. "And as luck would have it, I just happen to have a second pair of earphones."

Tara took the extra earphones and found that

the wires were just long enough to allow her and Kirby to waltz together as partners to the music of an easy-listening station. At first they kept tripping over each other's skates and getting the earphone wires tangled. But soon they got used to skating together and began moving along well.

Off the ice, Kirby was still not Tara's romantic ideal, but on skates he came closer. Before Tara knew it, she was lost in a daydream, imagining herself skating for the Olympic ice-dancing championship in a dazzling sequin-covered costume.

She was startled when Kirby finally broke into her reverie by turning down the volume of the music. "I guess we'd better be getting back," he said. "I think the others are trying to get our attention."

Across the ice, Tara could see Olivia waving to them. A tiny figure in a red sweater and red kiddy-style ear muffs, she could almost have passed for one of the children who'd been skating with their father earlier.

But the kids and their father were gone now. And so were the four college students. As she and Kirby skated back across the lake toward Olivia and the others, Tara noticed for the first time that the sun had dropped down behind the hill that lay just to the south of the pond. The two of them were casting long shadows on the ice, and the temperature had started to plummet.

"It seems like we were just skating for a few minutes." Tara sighed. "I wonder what time it is."

Olivia, who had skated out to meet them,

hadn't heard the question. But her first words provided an answer. "We'd better get going," she said in a worried voice. "It's four o'clock."

"Well, that's not so bad," Tara said, relieved. "It looks later than that."

"It's bad enough," Olivia answered. "We all need to get home and grab some dinner before the game."

"I didn't mean to stay so long myself," Kirby said. "I borrowed my brother's car for the afternoon, and I've got a couple of errands to do before I return it." He pointed toward the two-seater Subaru Brat that was parked a little ways up the road from the Chevy. "Any of you guys need a lift?"

"No, thanks," said Tara. "I've got plenty of room. Go ahead and do your errands."

"Okay. See you all at the game tonight," he said. "I'll be warming the bench as usual."

Kirby hurriedly changed into his shoes then sprinted up the snowy slope toward the Brat and drove away. It took Tara a little longer to get into her tight knee-high boots.

"Come on," Olivia said impatiently as Tara fussed over the task of zipping up her boots without catching her jeans in the zipper. Sean, meanwhile, had rolled a snowball, which he playfully lobbed in Olivia's direction. "Lighten up," he said. "You've been worried ever since we left home."

"I know. I just can't help it," Olivia acknowledged. "I just keep thinking of how steamed Coach Engborg would be if the whole squad was late for a game." But she smiled anyway, made a snowball of her own, and lobbed it back at Sean. Her aim was good and the snowball scored a solid hit on Sean's shoulder.

"I'm ready," Tara announced, "if you two can tear yourselves away from your snowball fight."

"Okay, we're coming. But there's no need to be so serious," Sean groused good-naturedly. "I'll tell you girls when it's time to worry."

They all trudged up the hill to the car. Sean jogged ahead of them, still playfully pelting them with soggy but harmless snowballs. Then he sprinted the last twenty yards or so toward the crest of the hill.

Seconds later, he was back at their sides. "I hate to say this," he announced, "but we've got a flat tire."

Tara's good mood dissolved instantly. "But that can't be!" she wailed. "I've only had that car a week."

Her protest was so irrational that everyone burst into laughter. "I'm afraid it doesn't work that way," Sean said. "Certainly not with used cars. But it's no great disaster. Give me the keys and I'll get the spare out of the trunk."

Sean sprinted back toward the Chevy, keys in hand. By the time the others reached him, he had the trunk open and had rolled the spare into position next to the flat. "I couldn't find the jack," he said to Tara. "Where is it kept on these cars?"

Tara looked blank. "Gee, I don't know," she said. "Isn't it in there?"

"Not that I can see. You do *have* a jack, don't you?"

"Naturally." But Tara looked panicky. "I mean all cars have a jack. So this one must, too. Right?"

Jessica and Olivia looked at each other and groaned. Sean just leaned the tire against a snow bank and stood up. "Remember me saying that I'd tell you girls when it was time to start worrying? Well, I think now's the time."

CHAPTER

They searched through the trunk and under the seats and even under the hood.

"It's no use," Jessica said finally. "Daniel, my stepdad, used to have a Chevy. I can guarantee you there's no secret compartment. That jack should be in the trunk."

"Can't we drive on the flat at least as far as the main road?" Tara asked.

Sean shook his head. "I don't think it's a good idea. For one thing, you'd probably damage the wheel. That tire's flat as a pancake. It's probably been leaking for a while."

"I thought the ride was a little rough on the way out here," said Olivia, who'd been riding in the backseat on the side of the flat. "I bet the tire was low even then."

"For another thing," Sean continued, "it's gotten a lot colder since we drove in here. I bet the road has turned icy in spots. I don't think we should risk an accident. We could get into a real mess trying to get through on three good tires. This is a rear-wheel drive car, too, isn't it?"

"I guess so," said Tara vaguely.

"How can anyone own a car and not know whether it's front-wheel drive or rear-wheel drive?" Hope asked in her most reasonable tone of voice. "For that matter, how can anyone drive without a jack? Especially in the country."

"Give me a break!" Tara snapped. "I've only had the car a few days. Besides, I know my father, and he would definitely not have given me a car that didn't have the right equipment. There must have been a jack."

"Fighting won't help us get out of here," Olivia put in. "It doesn't matter what happened. There's no jack now. The question is, what do we do next?"

"It's at least a couple of miles back to the road," Sean said. "But with luck, I can jog out there and flag down help before it gets dark."

"I'll go with you," Jessica said quickly. "Don't worry. I can keep up."

"If you three get really cold, I guess you could start the car and run the heater," Sean said to the others. "But whatever you do, put the top down, or open the windows. I don't want you to asphyxiate yourselves."

"I'm not a total idiot," Tara shot back. No one commented.

Hope watched Jessica and Sean trot up the road. "As long as it's still light," she said, "we might as well do some stretching exercises. They'll keep us warm. And if we do manage to make it to the game, at least we won't be too stiff to cheer."

"What do you mean, 'if'?" Olivia wailed. "We've got to make it." She turned toward Tara accusingly. "This is all your fault. And there's one 'if' I am sure of: *If* we don't make that game, I'll never forgive you."

It took thirty minutes of brisk jogging for Jessica and Sean to reach the main road. The distance was longer than Jessica had remembered, and she spent the last fifteen minutes trying to catch her breath. It was scant comfort that Sean was panting, too.

Still, she managed to stay even with Sean until the last hundred yards or so. Then Sean, catching sight of an approaching car, sprinted on ahead and stuck out his thumb.

The driver of the car took one look at him . . . and sped on past.

"Now I know why I came along," Jessica said, as soon as she'd recovered enough to talk. "This is a pretty lonely road. People will be more likely to stop if they see me."

Just as she finished speaking, an old model Honda Civic came into view. Jessica waved her arms, and the car slowed to a crawl, then stopped. The driver was a white-haired lady wearing wire-rimmed glasses. "Are you all right, dear?" she asked, her voice full of concern.

Jessica explained the problem, and the woman reached over to unlock the passenger-side doors. "I'm in a big hurry myself," she said. "I'm supposed to be the caller at the bingo game over in Rangely, and it starts in half an hour. But it won't hurt me to drop you at the gas station up the road."

Somehow, Jessica had imagined that the first motorist to come along would drive down to the pond, produce a jack, and help them fix the flat. Either that, or rescue all of them and whisk them off to Tarenton High in time for the game.

Now she realized that that had been a fantasy. The jack for this tiny car might not even fit the much bigger Chevy. In any case, there was no way that they could expect this lady to drive all the way down the deserted access road to the lake with two complete strangers.

Jessica sighed and hopped into the front seat. Sean, already settled in the back, must have read her mind. "Don't worry," he said, "we'll get help at the gas station."

But when they got to the station it turned out to consist of two weathered looking gas pumps in front of a convenience store. The lady let them out, then drove off at top speed, muttering about being late for her bingo.

Inside the store, the woman behind the counter looked blank when they asked for a mechanic. "There's just me working tonight," she said. "And I can't very well close up the store, can I? You'll have to call someone from town."

It was a quarter after five and already dark. Jessica debated calling on her older brother John, then realized that the chances of his being home at this hour on a Saturday were not good. Besides, he'd be sure to tell her mother and stepfather, and it would be just as well if they could deal with this without having any parents find out about it. On the other hand, no garage was going to worry about whether or not the squad made it to the game on time. The one person she knew could help was Patrick. Frantically, she dialed his work number.

"H & T's TLC Moving. We treat your valuables with tender, loving care," said a pleasant voice.

"Pres? Is that you?" Jessica asked. "Is Patrick around?"

" 'Fraid not. He went to move a piano to some-place up in Hargety County. I don't expect him back for an hour at least."

Hastily, Jessica explained the situation. She didn't even have to ask for Pres's help. "Just stay where you are," he told her. "I'll bring the panel truck."

It was twenty to six when Pres pulled up in front of the store where Jessica and Sean were waiting. Twelve minutes later — Jessica was checking her watch compulsively now — they were almost at the end of the Grover Pond access road, near the place where they had left the Chevy.

As they made the turn, they could see Olivia,

Hope, and Tara standing in the snow-dusted parking lot, doing a cheer routine by the light of the rising full moon.

Pres burst into laughter.

"I've got to hand it to you," he told them when they approached the truck. "I thought we were a dedicated squad, but you guys are something else."

"Dedication nothing," sniffed Olivia. "We were just trying to keep from stiffening up like boards. The minute I stop moving, my muscles are planing to go on strike."

"Don't let them do that yet," advised Pres. "You've still got a game to go to."

"If we can make it . . ." Sean said. "I predict that if we're not ready to take the floor at six-thirty the coach is going to blow a gasket. Either that or give up on cheerleading entirely. She had a pretty rough week, worrying about this Pompon Squad business."

"That's right," agreed Hope. "I'm sure she was under pressure from Mrs. Oetjen not to let the Pompon Squad spend its treasury on itself. But she decided to trust us to work things out. Now, if we let her down — "

"What do you mean, 'we'?" Jessica put in. "Tara's the one who talked us into this trip in the first place. Then she got us stranded here. . . ."

Up until now, Jessica had been too busy trying to solve their problem to feel any anger. But suddenly she felt the resentment rising up inside her in waves.

Pres leaned against the side of the truck, his arms crossed over his chest. "When you've decided to quit picking at each other, let me know," he told them.

"Pres is right," said Sean. "Let's not waste time on this now."

Jessica looked at her watch. It was already six o'clock. "But it's already too late," she wailed.

"Maybe not," said Olivia. "I don't know about the rest of you, but my uniform is in the locker room at school. We could go straight there."

"Mine, too," said Hope.

One by one, the others nodded. That in itself was a stroke of luck. Normally, at least some of the cheerleaders would have had taken their uniforms to the cleaners, or home to be pressed. It was only because of yesterday's pep rally that they'd all left them at school.

"Good," said Pres. "Then the first order of business is to get you all to the high school. Let's leave the car here for now. Patrick and I will come out later and one of us can drive it back to town."

Pres asked Jessica, who was still the most upset, to sit up front with him. The others piled into the back of the truck.

"It's probably just as well that Tara didn't have to drive you all up here," said Pres as he negotiated the icy curves on the access road.

"I'm sorry we put you to all this trouble," Jessica apologized.

"Oh, I don't mind. It reminds me of all the fun

I had last year. The squad had some great times. But somehow, it's the crises that I remember best of all. Those were the days!"

Jessica didn't find this very comforting. This was her life and she didn't consider the crises all that amusing. Furthermore, she couldn't help wondering if Patrick felt the same way Pres did. Maybe he had only started dating her out of nostalgia for his own senior year. What if she was just a substitute for his senior year love, Mary Ellen? If so, then it made sense that he'd be tempted to dump her the minute it seemed that Mary Ellen was willing to give him another chance.

She wanted in the worst way to ask Pres if he knew that Mary Ellen had been writing to Patrick. But this didn't seem to be the moment for it. Pres was going out of his way to be helpful. Why distract him by bringing up a touchy subject like that?

In the back of the van, Tara was doing her best to convince the others that this disaster wasn't all her fault. "I just know there must have been a jack in the car when I got it," she kept saying. "If it isn't there now, then someone took it."

Sean looked skeptical. "Why would anyone want to take your jack? And furthermore, how could anyone break into the trunk without the keys to your car?"

"I don't know. . . ."

"Then quit trying to shift the blame onto someone else," Sean said.

Thinking it over, Tara realized that it wasn't impossible that someone had taken her car keys. Like all the other girls, she had locked her purse in the coach's office during the rally yesterday. But she wasn't used to carrying her car keys yet, and she was in the careless habit of stuffing them into her pocket. Anyone could have slipped into the locker room and taken them, then returned them later.

But who would have known to find them there? The other members of the squad might, but of course they wouldn't take them. Kirby might have noticed, too. And Diana. . . . Tara remembered fishing her keys out of her pocket when she left Diana's house the other night.

"I know who did it!" she cried aloud. "That Diana Tucker just wanted revenge. She took Hope's music, too, and I knew about it."

"Don't be silly," said Hope. "My music turned up in the orchestra room. Besides, if you knew Diana took it, why would you wait until now to tell us about it?"

"I guess I just felt sorry for her . . ." Tara began. Even she knew that the truth did not sound very plausible.

"That's a laugh," Sean snorted. "No one has been more down on Diana than you, right from her first day in school. She may have her faults, but that's no excuse for trying to blame her for all this."

Tara was sure she was right, but she finally gave up trying to convince the others. She had tried to give Diana a break, and instead she'd walked right into her trap. Unless she had some evidence, there was no way now that the squad was going to take her word against anyone else's, even Diana's.

CHAPTER

 15

Peter Rayman stepped out of the shower and wrapped himself in the blue terrycloth bathrobe that had been a Christmas gift from his father. He would have to be ready to start for school in half an hour, and he still wasn't sure how he was going to act when he came face-to-face with the rest of the squad.

All afternoon long, he had been thinking longingly about the skating party. He was sure the other kids must have been having a great time out there at Grover's Pond, and it drove him half crazy to think that he was being left out.

It only made matters worse that he couldn't decide who to blame. Tara *had* invited him, after all. But he couldn't help suspecting that she had only asked him because she expected him to use the occasion to make up with Hope. None of

144

the other cheerleaders let the squad run their love life. How had he ever gotten himself into this fix?

Peter reached inside the top drawer of his dresser and fumbled under a pile of T-shirts for the framed photograph of his father that he kept there. He wasn't exactly hiding it. He knew his mother wouldn't mind him keeping his dad's picture. It just seemed more tactful to keep it where she wouldn't have to see it every time she came into the room.

Looking at the picture now, Peter couldn't help thinking how much he was starting to look like his father. They both had the same wiry good looks and sandy-colored hair. Their faces even wore the same sensitive, thoughtful expression.

If only his dad was around now, Peter thought, he could tell him how to handle the fix he was in!

But his father had not been a part of Peter's life for a long time. He was living in California with his second wife and a new set of children. Peter had to make do with an occasional phone call and presents on his birthday and at Christmas.

He even wondered whether his dad picked out those presents himself. It was hard to imagine his father thinking that a bathrobe would make an appropriate gift for his son! A robe seemed more like the kind of thing the second Mrs. Rayman would choose for the child of her husband's first marriage: useful, impersonal, and unlikely to be returned because it didn't fit.

One thing you had to give the old man credit for, he hadn't let guilt run his life. Why should his son be any different? Feeling defiant, Peter picked up the phone and made arrangements to meet Diana before the game.

He arrived at the school at about six o'clock and found Diana waiting for him in the front hall. She looked great as usual, dressed in her fur jacket, form-fitting corduroy pants, and lizard-look boots. But her mood was even stranger than it had been the day before. She seemed nervous and snappish one minute and giddy with elation the next.

"Is anything wrong?" he asked after Diana had gone through her third mood swing in as many minutes.

"Of course there's nothing wrong," she snapped. "Can't I be happy if I want to be?"

Then, turning all smiles again, she gave him a hurried but passionate kiss on the lips. "Maybe it's being around you that gets me acting crazy like this. I have a feeling this is going to be an important evening for us, Peter."

Peter blinked in surprise. He wasn't used to having that effect on women. But why knock it?

They entered the school arm in arm and found Coach Engborg pacing nervously in the hall in front of the gym entrance. Peter knew he was a few minutes late. The coach had wanted the squad to be present and changed by six o'clock so they'd have time to warm up before the game started. But he had purposely tried to be the last to arrive so that he wouldn't have to listen to everyone's stories about the skating party.

"Sorry, Coach . . ." he began. "Didn't mean to

worry you, but I guess someone has to be last."

"Last!" Ardith Engborg exclaimed. "You're the first! I was hoping you could tell me when I could expect your colleagues to show up."

"They were all together this afternoon," Peter told her. "They went skating. But I'm sure they wouldn't be late getting back unless something was seriously wrong."

This was hardly reassuring. So far, Mrs. Engborg had been annoyed. Now she was beginning to get really worried. The country roads around Tarenton could turn slick and dangerous on short notice. Visions of an automobile accident flashed in front of her eyes.

The coach was dressed for the game in a neat tweed skirt, a sweater, and nylon stockings, an outfit that contrasted incongruously with the battered running shoes she wore on her feet. As she stood talking to Peter, her fears were betrayed by her inability to keep her feet still. "I'll give those kids until six-thirty on the nose," she said as she paced in front of the gym door. "But if they aren't here by the starting whistle, I'm going to call the highway patrol."

Mrs. Engborg went back into the gym, and Peter asked Diana to stand lookout in the hall while he changed into his uniform.

When he returned a couple of minutes later, Diana had no news. "I don't know why the coach is so worried," she said. "I'm sure there hasn't been an accident."

"How can you be so sure?" he asked.

Diana avoided the question with a knowing toss

of the head. "Oh, you know that bunch. They were probably having so much fun they forgot the time."

This was exactly what Peter was thinking. No doubt the group would show up when they were good and ready. And in the meantime, he had probably missed out on some fantastic adventure that everyone would be talking about for a week.

"It isn't fair to you," Diana said, reading his mind. "I mean, they can hardly expect you to go out there and cheer by yourself."

She flashed a mischievous grin. "I have an idea! Why don't I fill in for them? I know enough to fake most of the routines."

Peter could think of a million reasons why this was the worst idea he'd heard in a long time. But he only offered one, the best one he could think of: "For one thing, Coach would never allow it," he warned.

"Who cares about her?" Diana pouted. "I don't see what would be such a big deal about my filling in in an emergency."

"We don't know that there's an emergency. They'll probably show up any minute now."

"Somehow I don't think so."

Peter wondered fleetingly why Diana was so sure of this. But the thought was pushed out of his mind by the need to talk her out of this notion of playing substitute. "Another reason you can't do it," he pointed out, "is that you don't have a uniform."

Diana was unfazed. "I'm sure Tara's will fit me. She couldn't possibly mind my borrowing it."

"Oh no?"

Diana gave his arm a knowing squeeze. "Don't be such a party pooper. I'm sure that once the coach sees that I'm ready to step in, she'll agree that it's a good idea. We'll have a great time, too. Don't you want to cheer with me?"

"This is just going to get us in trouble. . . ."

Peter's words trailed off as he realized that he was talking to himself. Diana was already striding away from him, heading for the hall entrance to the girls' locker room. He watched dumbfounded as she marched through the door and out of sight.

Peter stayed in the hall, trying to figure out his next move. Maybe Diana was right. Maybe he was acting like a wimp. Diana had so much confidence that she might even be able to get away with this. On the other hand, he couldn't help thinking that somehow he was going to end up taking the blame for her antics.

There was really nothing he could do except go inside and warn the coach. But that seemed like a childish move — playing tattletale.

He was still standing in the hall, trying to plan his next move, when the rest of the squad came running in from outside. Sean immediately sprinted off to the boys' locker room. The girls headed in the opposite direction, toward Peter.

"It's six-twenty-five," Jessica was all but shrieking. "I hope you're satisfied, Tara. If it wasn't for Pres, we'd have missed the game completely."

"Can't you two stop arguing?" Hope wailed.

Olivia was the first to catch sight of Peter. "Go in and tell Coach we're here," she told him. "If I

149

know the coach, she's probably ready to call out the bloodhounds by now."

"No, just the highway patrol," he corrected her.

Then he remembered that Diana was inside the locker room. "Wait a second. Don't go in there yet," he told the girls. "I've got to tell you something first. . . ."

But he didn't get the chance. At that moment, Diana came prancing through the door, dressed in Tara's red and white uniform. "See!" she said grabbing Peter's arm. "I told you it would be okay. We're all set!"

Tara, Olivia, Jessica, and Hope gasped in unison at Diana's appearance.

Olivia found her voice first. "What's the meaning of this?" she shouted. "Since when are you a member of the squad, Diana Tucker?"

Diana faced her squarely, her hands on her hips. "Maybe I *should* be. At least *I* was here. I was here. I didn't come waltzing in the door five minutes before game time."

Tara was sure now that she had been right in blaming Diana for her car troubles. "I knew this was your fault," she accused. "No one would believe me, but I was right all along. You sabotaged my car."

"I don't know what you're talking about," Diana said.

"Oh yes you do!"

Diana was doing a good job of looking like an injured innocent. "I do not. How can it be my fault? I can't help it if you had a flat tire and no jack to fix it with."

150

Hope glared at her but she kept her voice level. "Wait a second! How did you know we had a flat tire? We never said anything about a flat tire. Or about not having a jack either! You knew because you're responsible! Right?"

Hope's quiet, steady tone of voice only made her anger more impressive. "Furthermore, Tara was right when she said you were the one who took my music. I didn't believe you could be such a snake. But I was wrong, wasn't I?"

"You can't prove that."

"We'll see about that after the game," Olivia told her. "In the meantime, I think you'd better get out of that uniform. And be quick about it, too."

The sight of Olivia facing down the much taller Diana would have been funny if Olivia hadn't been in such total command of the situation. Diana knew she had been bested, and the defiance drained out of her instantly. "I didn't mean to get all of you in trouble," she protested feebly. "How was I to know that the rest of you would be in the car when Tara's tire finally went flat?"

This almost set Tara off again, but Olivia managed to shepherd all the girls into the locker room. She stationed Tara with Hope and Jessica at one end, and stood in front of Diana's cubicle until Tara's uniform was handed out to her. "Now get dressed and get out of here," she told Diana. "I still have a few words I want to say to you, but they'll have to wait until after the game."

Peter, meanwhile, was still trying to recover

from the shock of what he'd just learned. At the moment Hope accused Diana of stealing her music, he suddenly recalled the music he'd seen lying on the floor of Diana's locker. That had been the very day Hope's music was taken!

He'd been a fool not to make the connection before now. But, of course, he hadn't wanted to even imagine that Diana was a thief. He'd known that she liked to have her own way, but he hadn't dreamed she was capable of anything like that.

"How could I have let a girl make such a dummy out of me?" he asked Sean.

"What's the big deal?" Sean asked with a shrug. "Women make dummies out of me all the time."

Peter couldn't help laughing. What Sean said was true, even though he'd never thought about it before. Sean had a lot of success with girls, but he also ended up acting foolish a lot. Peter saw now that he could never manage to copy Sean's devil-may-care approach to life. He'd been wrong even to try.

CHAPTER

16

Inside the gym, Ardith Engborg was having a conference with the referee. The start of the game had already been delayed several minutes, but now she was giving the go-ahead signal.

"Are you sure you don't want me to wait a few more minutes?" the ref asked her.

"That wouldn't be fair to the players. They're here ready to go, and so are the Deep River cheerleaders. If my people can't get here on time that's their problem."

The ref shook his head, and motioned to the coaches to get the teams ready for the opening jump shot.

The coach made a beeline for her office. On her way, she was stopped by Olivia's boyfriend, David Duffy. He had finished his bowling story early and come on over to catch the game.

"I know that Olivia would be here on time if it were physically possible," he told the coach. "I'm definitely ready to start worrying."

"So am I," Coach Engborg agreed. "I'm going to call the police right now."

No sooner had the coach disappeared than Olivia, Hope, Jessica and Tara came running out of their locker room. Sean and Peter, who had been waiting outside in the hall, ran to join them. Duffy made eye contact with Olivia and blew her a kiss, then ran off to give the news to Ardith Engborg. He caught her just as she was about to dictate an all points bulletin to the highway patrol.

Olivia grabbed her megaphone and shouted to the home fans section:

"Got the spirit?
Let's hear it!"

There was a tremendous answering roar.

For a minute or so, Peter found himself wondering whether he did have the spirit. Or if he could even manage to fake it. The last thing he felt like doing was cheering.

Olivia could see that the whole squad was a little bit distracted. She decided to get them into the swing of things by starting off with some of the old familiar cheers, the ones they could all do in their sleep if necessary.

"We've got the T-E-A-M," she shouted,
"That's on the B-E-A-M. . . ."

The cheer was almost too familiar. As it approached its end, Peter had a second of panic. He'd been moving on automatic pilot, but all of a sudden he couldn't remember the final move. Had the squad been ending that cheer with a straddle jump or a herky? If he did a different move from everyone else he was going to look ridiculous.

On the second repetition of the line "Skin 'em alive," he leaped into a straddle jump, really giving it his all. It was a great jump, high and cleanly executed. One of his best ever. Unfortunately, it was not the right jump.

The gaffe set off a round of giggles in the cheering section. Peter felt the anger he'd been trying to deal with all week long coming to a boil. He started to turn and walk off the court, and was startled when Tara grabbed his arm. "It happens to all of us," she said, giving him a reassuring smile. "Don't let it bother you."

Peter had never felt especially close to Tara. He'd always thought of her as fun and flamboyant, but not the type to reach out to offer help to anyone else. And certainly not to him. "I guess you're right," he acknowledged.

For the next few cheers, Tara managed to stay next to him, giving him a subtle cue now and then and once, when he did a good back flip, flashing the thumbs up sign.

He was starting to feel like part of the team again. If only Hope would change her mind about him, everything might yet work out. So far, he and Hope hadn't had any partner stunts to do together, but they were paired off during the pompon routine. Peter knew that the routine was going to be no fun for either of them unless he could manage to talk to Hope before then.

At the beginning of the halftime break, he finally got his chance. Deep River had brought its own cheerleaders, a squad of six girls who were loud and enthusiastic if not on the same level of skill as Tarenton. Out of courtesy, they were given a chance to take over the court first and do their routines.

In the meantime, the Tarenton squad gathered on the sidelines, watching politely and taking the chance to catch their breath. Hope had taken a seat on one of the team benches and was using the time to retie the laces on one of her shoes. Peter immediately sat down next to her. "I've got to talk to you," he said.

Hope frowned. "Now? Can't it wait until after the game?"

"I just wanted you to know that I'm sorry," Peter pressed on. "I'm not saying that none of it was my fault. But I kind of got caught up in Diana's plans. It all happened so fast."

The whole time he was talking, Hope seemed to be studying her shoes. Peter was sure she was going to tell him to get lost permanently. Instead, she surprised him.

"Yesterday, I would have said that blaming Diana was a complete cop-out, but today I'm not so sure. After all, she even fooled Tara.

"Maybe I even owe Diana a vote of thanks," she added.

This was the last thing Peter had expected. "I don't get it."

"I've been thinking about how upset I was over that lost sheet music," she explained. "It shouldn't have been a major crisis. But I just couldn't stand the thought that I'd made a mistake. I guess I have this habit of thinking that the whole world will end if my life isn't perfectly in control. I keep thinking that no one will like me anymore if they know I've failed. . . ."

"But that's crazy," Peter said. "You haven't failed at anything. And even if you did, no one would stop liking you."

"I know. So from now on, I'm going to try not to be so tough on myself. Or on other people, for that matter."

"Does that mean we're back together again?" Peter wondered.

"I'm not sure."

Hope might have said more, but the opening notes of the squad's halftime music interrupted her. "Let's just go out and enjoy the routine," she said, grabbing her pompons.

As the cheering section launched into its version of "Alexander's Ragtime Band," the squad performed flawlessly, beginning with a series of jumps and then moving on to some stunts that included the butterfly lift that Peter and Hope had practiced without much success earlier in the week.

But Hope's change of heart had certainly improved her timing. Peter had no trouble holding her above his head. Hope was moving so well that she seemed almost weightless, as if she could have soared without any help at all. And her smile did not seem merely polite. She looked vibrant.

Olivia and Jessica both noticed the change right away.

"It looks as if Hope must have made up with Peter," Jessica observed as they left the floor after the end of the routine.

"I guess so," Olivia agreed. "But I think the squad deserves some credit, too. We bring out the best in each other."

Even the game picked up in the second half. Tarenton had been trailing Deep River by at least a half dozen points through the first two periods. But in the second half, the Wolves changed to a one-on-one defense and started to have some success blocking Deep River's shots. Gradually, the gap narrowed. Tarenton was behind by only three points, when its star center fouled out of the game.

His departure was greeted by groans and cat-calls. The home side was almost ready to concede defeat — except for Tara, who whooped with joy when she saw Kirby being sent onto the floor.

In spite of Kirby's all-round athletic ability, he was a confirmed bench jockey when it came to basketball. He hardly ever got to play unless Tarenton already had a commanding lead.

Kirby's performance over the next few plays showed why. He missed an easy lay-up shot. Then, seconds later, he let a pass get away from him.

With thirty seconds left to play, Tarenton managed to close its deficit to one point. The crowd's noise was deafening. And Tara noticed that she was clutching her pompons so hard that her knuckles had turned white.

Tarenton had the ball, but its best scorers couldn't manage to get a clear shot at the basket. The Deep River cheerleaders were calling out the seconds on the clock: "Ten . . . nine . . . eight . . . seven. . . ."

With four seconds to go, Kirby was backed up in the corner, desperately looking for a teammate inside to pass to.

"Three . . . two . . ." chanted the Deep River squad.

"Shoot it, Kirby," screamed Tara.

With no time left to set up a play, Kirby did just that. His quick charge followed by a one-handed shot caught the Deep River guards off balance. The ball teetered on the lip of the basket as if trying to make up its own mind whether or not to reward Kirby's awkward but aggressive move.

The Tarenton fans held their breath. Then the ball dropped through the net as the buzzer sounded.

"Way to go! We did it!" screamed Sean. The crowd exploded with joy, and Sean hoisted Olivia on his shoulders so that she could be seen as she led the victory cheer.

Tara impulsively raced onto the court and gave Kirby a big hug.

In spite of the fact that they had just spent the afternoon skating together, Kirby looked surprised and even a little unhappy at the attention.

Instinctively, Tara drew back. "Congratulations on a good game," she said, almost formally.

"Thanks." Kirby's eyes met hers for a second and then moved away.

Tara retreated to join Peter and Hope on the sidelines. "What did I do?" she wondered aloud.

"Maybe he's just shy," suggested Hope. "It's one thing to talk to you outside of school. But it's something else to have you make a big fuss over him here in front of half the student body and all his teammates. Kirby isn't used to being in the spotlight. And after all, you are one of the most popular girls at Tarenton High."

Tara sighed. Sometimes life was complicated. Who would ever have thought that there was such a thing as being too popular?

In her confusion over Kirby, Tara had almost forgotten about the problems of earlier in the evening. But Mrs. Engborg certainly hadn't. As soon as the crowd began to file out of the gym, she called the squad into her office.

"I know you all want to celebrate tonight's win," she began, "but I think we have something to discuss."

The cheerleaders exchanged nervous glances. They all wanted to talk about the trouble Diana had caused, but telling tales on an outsider didn't come easy. It was especially hard since everyone knew that the coach hated excuses.

Mrs. Engborg herself finally broke the silence. "Maybe it would save time if I told you that I've already had a long talk with Diana myself. She admitted stealing the jack from Tara's car after the pep rally yesterday. She also tried to cut her tire by jamming a nail file into it. But the file broke off and she was sure she had failed. Later, the piece of file that was stuck in the tire must have worked its way out and caused the tire to develop a slow leak.

"Diana had no way of knowing that the tire would go flat when it did and almost keep all of you from getting to the game. Her scheme worked even better than she expected, but she was also pretty shaken up by it. She started to worry that for once she had gone too far. After all, sabotaging people's cars can be a dangerous business."

"It sure can," said Sean. "She deserves to be suspended from school, at the very least."

"That's what I wanted to talk to you about," Mrs. Engborg continued. "If you people decide to make an issue of this, I wouldn't be surprised if Diana *is* suspended."

"If? . . ." Olivia sputtered. "Why shouldn't we make an issue of it? That girl is a menace. She stole Hope's music, too. Besides being guilty of vandalism."

"Diana's impulsive behavior has gotten her into trouble before," the coach said. "But she's also had a tough life. That girl has never lived in one place long enough to attend the same school for an entire year. Her father's job keeps him moving from place to place. And the present Mrs. Tucker isn't Diana's real mother, either. She's something like her third stepmother."

Tara thought of the nervous woman who had greeted her when she visited Diana at home. No wonder she had acted so strangely. It couldn't be easy having Diana as a stepdaughter. "So what are you suggesting?" she asked.

"After I talked to Diana, I called the counselor who has been working with her," Mrs. Engborg said. "He thinks Diana will never change as long as she keeps moving from school to school and place to place. So he asked whether we'd consider giving Diana another chance."

"No way!" Olivia was indignant. "Other people have problems, too, but they don't go around stealing and cutting tires. Why should Diana get special treatment?"

Olivia looked around the group, sure that everyone would agree with her. She was shocked to see Hope shaking her head.

"In one way you're right," Hope said. "But maybe it wouldn't be so terrible to give her a second chance. As for her taking my music, that wouldn't have been such a big deal if I had had the courage to tell Mr. Martin about it right away. So I vote to let her stay."

"I'll go along with that," Peter said softly. He was furious with Diana, but after all he'd been the one who was dating her. And if Hope was in favor of dropping the subject, he didn't want to be the one keeping it alive.

"I'm with Olivia," said Sean. "I think it's crazy to let this go."

Jessica just shrugged. "I don't know who's right," she said. "I wasn't one of the chief victims, anyway. So I guess I abstain."

Everyone looked at Tara.

Why me? she asked herself. It was true that it was her car Diana had vandalized. But she hated to be the deciding vote.

It occurred to her, though, that if her parents had to hear the entire story of today's events, they might want to take her car away. It wouldn't matter that she hadn't been at fault. They'd be so worried that they'd want to keep her home for the rest of the semester for her own protection.

For another thing, Tara felt that she was the only member of the group who could understand Diana's motives. Diana was desperate for attention, and as long as she kept on getting it by causing trouble, she would go right ahead. Probably the worst punishment anyone could give someone like her was to deprive her of her chance to be the center of attention.

"I vote to give her another chance," she said finally. "Anyway, now that we all know what Diana is like, I don't see how she can expect to get away with her little schemes."

Olivia rolled her eyes in exasperation. "I hope you're right," she told Tara. "I don't agree, but if that's what the group wants, I'll go along with it."

CHAPTER

When the girls finished changing into their street clothes, they found Pres and Patrick waiting for them in the front hall. Pres was holding the key to Tara's car, which he dropped into her hand.

"It's parked right outside," he said. "And everything's in good order. We got the tire fixed at the garage we use for our trucks, and the guy threw in a jack for free." He laughed. "That's one of the benefits of being a pillar of the business community."

Tara thanked Pres effusively, then took off with Hope and Peter in tow. She had promised to give them a lift to Dopey's, and her mind was already focused on trying to get outside in time to meet Kirby before he left school.

In his way, Kirby was almost more of a mystery

to her than Diana was. She had no idea what went on in the minds of shy people, and she felt challenged to get Kirby to go out with her in public at least once. Perhaps if she offered him a lift when Hope and Peter were along, he wouldn't feel that he was being invited out on an official date.

Olivia left the group next, arm in arm with Duffy. Then Sean came out of the boys' locker room and stopped over to thank Pres for his help before heading out to his own car.

Soon Jessica was left standing with Pres and Patrick. "I know I said thanks already," she told Pres, "but I want to tell you again how nice it was of you to come right out and get us."

"Think nothing of it. Besides, it's going to make a good story to tell Mary Ellen when she's around again."

"Around?" As Jessica's lips formed the question, she couldn't help staring at Patrick to see how he reacted to Mary Ellen's name.

Pres didn't seem to notice. "It isn't one hundred percent certain yet, but Mary Ellen is thinking about moving back here."

"That's nice." Mary Ellen's return was the last thing Jessica wanted. She could hardly believe that she was standing there like a zombie, pretending that she thought it would be nice.

Turning to Patrick, she said, "I suppose you knew about this already. But you didn't tell me about it."

"I've been trying to, but it isn't easy to talk about and you sure didn't give me an opportunity.

That's what that letter was about that Mary Ellen wrote to me. You might say it was a 'Dear John' letter."

"Dear John?" It took her a second to think of what a "Dear John" letter was. When she did she wasn't completely reassured. "Oh, right," she said.

"Don't you believe me?"

"I believe you. But tell me, Patrick, how many times did Mary Ellen break up with you? As I remember, that never had any effect on your feelings at all. If anything, you were more hung up on her after every time."

Pres was starting to look as if he couldn't wait to make his escape.

Watching Pres and Patrick together, Jessica couldn't help but think how different they were. Pres's good looks were clean and angular. Even dressed in an old flannel shirt and much-washed chinos, Pres was incapable of looking sloppy. His dark-blond hair looked glossy and carefully blow-dried. And his teeth were so perfect. No matter how casually Pres chose to dress, those teeth showed that he came from a family that had never once had to stint on dentist bills.

Under his smooth exterior, Pres was actually warm and even a little sentimental. He loved Tarenton and he was tremendously loyal to his friends. But he hated shows of emotion. Jessica could see that he was almost desperate to get away from this conversation.

Patrick, on the other hand, was a bundle of intensity. Jessica had no doubt that he had loved Mary Ellen madly, or that he was absolutely sincere when he said that now that romance was finished. But did even Patrick know where his heart was going to lead him next?

"He's telling the truth," Pres said. "I'm the one Mary Ellen has been writing to. Writing love letters, I mean."

That put matters in a different light. Jessica could see from the pleading look in Patrick's eyes that it was true. Maybe Mary Ellen was really out of Patrick's life for good.

"I believe you," said Jessica to Pres, without taking her eyes off Patrick.

Pres seemed immensely relieved that his presence was no longer required. He stopped shifting his weight from one foot to the other. "Okay, good. I'll be moving on then. Maybe I'll see you all at Dopey's later on."

After Pres left, Patrick put a loving arm around her shoulders. His touch was gentle, but at the same time so possessive that Jessica felt her willpower ebbing away. No wonder Mary Ellen had spent half her time mesmerized by Patrick and the other half trying to break it off. She worried herself that Patrick's love might take over her whole life.

"I was ready to talk to you about that letter any time," Patrick said. "I don't understand why you didn't want to hear about it. After all, I didn't let your flirtation with Charles in New Orleans come between us."

"I know. I guess jealousy isn't always rational. Besides, sometimes I think I'm more scared when it looks as if things are working out. I'm afraid

I'll get so wrapped up in you that I'll be completely dependent."

Patrick whistled softly, forcing the air through that natural space between his front teeth that made his smile so irresistibly sexy. "Why do I always end up with girls who are afraid of commitment? Why me?"

Jessica had some theories about that. For one thing, Patrick's desire for commitment was so apparent that it would have scared off a lot of girls. On the other hand, she couldn't deny that she was a lot more cautious than most. But, then, girls ready for the kind of commitment Patrick wanted just didn't interest him.

That was one dilemma that wasn't going to be resolved any time soon. "I am ready to commit myself to going out with you tonight," she said lightly, her green eyes gazing into Patrick's blue ones. "Are you going to ask me, or not?"

"Oh, definitely."

Fortunately, Patrick and Pres had gone back to the garage to get Pres's Porsche after delivering Tara's car, so Patrick still had the panel truck. Jessica hardly needed help to get up the step into the passenger seat, but she didn't protest when Patrick swept her up in his arms and lifted her onto the step. Before letting go, he kissed her — a long, melting kiss that seemed to go on forever.

Twenty minutes later, they arrived at Dopey's, the kiss over but definitely not forgotten.

Jessica smiled as she pointed out Hope, Peter, and Tara seated at one of the front booths along with Kirby Hopkins. Her auburn hair hanging loose under a French beret of cream-colored wool, Tara looked more sultry than ever. Kirby was obviously interested, in a speechless sort of way. It seemed that Tara was doing much of the talking, with Hope intervening from time to time to try to draw him into the conversation.

"It looks like Tara managed to snare Kirby, after all," Jessica commented.

Patrick grinned. "I wouldn't bet on that relationship lasting too long. But it's certainly going to be an educational experience for Tara to be the pursuer and not the pursued."

A few minutes later, Olivia and Duffy emerged from the back room. Olivia stopped on her way out to compliment Holly Hudson on the Pompon Squad's turnout at the game and to thank her for writing the lyrics to the new pompon song.

Duffy, usually the king of wisecracks and the last to leave any gathering, was looking at Olivia with tender concern. "We probably shouldn't," he said when Olivia suggested stopping to join Jessica and Patrick for another soda. "You've had a tiring day. Besides, I promised your mother that we wouldn't be late. And this time, I want to show her that I'm capable of being trustworthy, if only for the sake of keeping her confused.

"Mrs. Evans can't decide whether I'm the sensible big-brother type or a cad and a rake of the first order," Duffy explained to Jessica and Patrick with a mock leer. "Naturally, I'm doing my best to make sure she never discovers my true nature."

Olivia had started to argue that she wasn't the least bit tired and was ready to stay out at least another hour, but Duffy's humor defeated her. "Okay," she agreed, "I guess it has been quite a day."

No sooner had they departed than Sean Dubrow made his entrance, surrounded by three junior girls. Waving a brisk hello to the other members of the squad, Sean and his fan club proceeded to a table in the back where he sat diplomatically across from the trio, basking in their undivided attention without ever giving a definite sign that he was favoring one of the three over the others.

"Sean could probably use the opposite kind of educational experience from Tara, but he isn't likely to try it," Jessica sighed. "Still, behind the Great Lover image, Sean is actually likable."

Patrick looked alarmed. "Don't tell me you're starting to fall for Dubrow?" he protested. "I couldn't stand losing another girl to the lover-boy type."

Patrick's admission of insecurity touched Jessica more than anything he had said all evening. "Of course not," she said, squeezing his hand reassuringly. "I was just thinking how surprising it is that the squad manages to get along in spite of our different personalities. You'd think that if you locked the six of us in a room together for twenty-four hours we'd end up enemies. Yet when some outsider tries to divide us, the experience always seems to bring us closer together."

"That," said Patrick, "is known as teamwork."

He held onto her hand, firmly but gently. "Teamwork doesn't work only for cheerleading squads, you know. I keep trying to convince you that you and I could be quite a team."

Jessica was beginning to realize that she, too, was tired from her long, eventful day. She felt warm and secure in Patrick's company, almost secure enough to tell him that he had succeeded in making her fall deeply in love with him. But surely this was something she ought to save for another occasion, when her judgment wasn't clouded by exhaustion and they were in a more romantic setting than a vinyl-upholstered booth at Dopey's.

"I'm not ready to give you the promise you're looking for," she told Patrick. "But whatever you do, don't give up on me. I'm definitely interested in being convinced."

"That's good enough for now, Jessica," he said, lightly caressing her shining hair. "But someday you're going to have to make a decision. Cheerleading doesn't last forever, and after that there's a big, complicated world out there."

Jessica knew it was true, but at the moment she was in no hurry to face that. Running up that lonely country road earlier in the evening with Sean, she'd felt that rescuing the squad from missing a game was the most important mission in the world. And later, cheering with them during the game against Deep River, she'd felt as happy as she'd ever been.

Whatever troubles they might have, the squad was not going to let her down. They were almost like a family. She just didn't know if she could ever trust Patrick in quite that way.

But why should she ruin her time of happiness by worrying about that? Cheerleading was her world right now, and the future Patrick kept trying to remind her of was far away.

Tara has never been able to be serious about anyone — until she falls in love with the wrong guy. Read Cheerleaders #29, FALLING IN LOVE.